DEATH AT THE HOWARD

A Jake Katz Novel
Dave Tevelin

For Sandy,

Muse, Wife,

Love of my life

DEATH AT THE HOWARD

March 27, 1958

Sam Katz dialed Operator and gave her the number.

"That'll be twenty-five cents for the first three minutes."

He dug into his pocket and muttered "*Ganefs*," the Yiddish term for thieves.

"Excuse me?," she said.

"I said 'I got it'," he said, and pushed five nickels into the slot. He heard the beeps as she dialed up Fanny. She'd let it ring three times, then he'd hang up. If she didn't hear a fourth ring, she knew to make dinner for just her and Jake and they'd save the quarter. So he wasn't happy to hear a pickup on the first ring.

"Hello?"

A quarter shot to hell, but for his son, it was worth it.

"Jakie? It's pop."

"Hi, pop. Where are you?"

"I'm in Trenton and I still got some work to do. I won't be home for dinner."

"Oh" was all Jake said but it was enough for Sam to hear the disappointment. Twelve, but still his daddy's boy.

"Are you studying your *haftorah*?" The bar-mitzvah was more than two months away but Sam knew who he was dealing with. If he and Fanny didn't stay on him day and night, he'd never get it down.

"I did it with the rabbi at Hebrew school."

"That's good. How did you do?"

"I don't know. Okay, I guess."

"You'll study more tonight, okay?"

No answer.

"Jake?"

"What?"

Sam pictured him, a shorter version of his own short self, sitting on the sofa, mesmerized by the television. Same

1

crew cut sandy brown hair, full nose, and big chin, but his mother's sparkling blue eyes. The ladies would go for that.

"Okay, *tateleh*," he said, "let me speak to your mother."

"Mom!," he heard him call, seeing him holding the phone out to his mother, then her, barely taller than Jake, fluttering in from the kitchen, wiping her hands on her apron.

"So, *nu*?," she said.

"So *nu* I'm not going to be home for dinner. I got one more visit to make, then I'll be back, maybe by eight?"

"Have you eaten?"

"I'll get a slice of pizza somewhere. I'll be fine."

"All right. You take care of yourself. I'll see you then."

"See you then."

He knew exactly where he was going for the pizza, right around the corner to De Lorenzo's on Hudson, the best pizza in Trenton. He pushed the door open and waved at the pretty lady behind the counter.

"Sophie, you doll, how've you been?"

"Great, Sam. Been a while. How're you?"

"Busy, busy, same as always. How's Chick?"

"Good. He's in the kitchen. What can we make you?"

"White clam, small."

She winked at him and wrote it up. Fanny kept a kosher house so his only chance to eat a little *traif* was when he was out and about on his own. He knew she knew but neither one of them ever said a word about it. Just another reason why he loved her so.

He slipped out of his overcoat and laid it on the thin red cushion at one side of the nearest booth, then slid in the other side to face the street. He pushed the table away to make some more room and stretched his legs. They barely reached the other side. He was what the Jews called a *bulvan* – a big-shouldered, thick-waisted anvil of a guy. More importantly, he wasn't afraid to mix it up. All that served him well when he knocked on doors to collect. He got into it back at Northeast High in Philly, whenever his uncle the kosher butcher needed some muscle to get paid. The word spread quick about this hard-assed, low-overhead Jew who could deliver the goods and business grew enough that they could move out to Levittown where they could afford for Fanny to stay home and raise their boy.

He pulled a lined sheet of notebook paper from his suit jacket pocket and unfolded it. The next call was on Emory so he could keep the car where it was. Gino Formaroli at 27. The guy owed Dunham's $10.35 for some lady's jewelry he bought on credit. Shouldn't take long, he thought.

He tucked the paper back in his pocket and watched two Negro kids about Jake's age ride their bikes down the sidewalk across the street, one a little brown butterball, the other one long and lean. He never saw a *schwarze* in the Burg before. It made him think of last summer when the Myers family moved into the Dogwood section on the other side of Levittown, maybe three miles from where he lived. They were a lot like his own family, a father with a job and a mother who stayed home to raise their kids. The only difference was they were colored.

The hue and cry that went up made him sick to his stomach. People marching day and night outside the house, screaming at them to get out, police guarding them, on the national news yet. And these weren't just *goyim* on the streets, but Jews too. A true *shondah*, a disgrace to his people. Jews, who should know something about being the outsiders, the hunted, the victims, Jews marching and writing to the newspapers to keep the colored out. Even his own so-

3

called friends, people who went to Beth El or Temple Shalom to worship God every *shabbos*, called him *schwarze-lover*. He marched too, but with the group who wanted the Myers to know that not all their neighbors were filled with hate and fear.

The pizza brought him back to De Lorenzo's.

"Here you go," Sophie said. "You ought to try the red one of these days. Even better."

Sam waved a finger up and down his gray plaid suit jacket.

"Can't afford to stain it. You know what dry cleaners charge?"

"I know. You want something to drink with that?"

"Coca-Cola'd be good."

She patted him on the shoulder. "Mangia!"

He glanced at his watch. Twenty to seven. He needed to hustle it up if he wanted to catch Formaroli home for dinner. He caught Sophie's eye and drew a check in the air. She brought it over with the bottle.

"You're in a hurry!" she said.

"Still got some business to take care of," he got out between bites. He jammed it all down, but left half the Coke. There was no bathroom at DeLorenzo's and it'd be an hour before he made it back home. He ran a napkin over his mouth and left two bucks on the table. Sophie could keep the change. By ten of, he was out the door.

He let out a good stiff belch that cleared his mind. Sam knew most people had a low opinion of what he did for a living but he liked it. It was a tough business and he could be a tough guy but his usual shtick was to turn on the charm, ask for just a little to make the store happy, then set up a schedule so the guy could catch up.

He crossed Swan and made a left at the next block till he saw 27 by the door of a little two-story white clapboard across the street. He walked past, then crossed the street a few doors up the block. It was dark out now so the lights were on. When he got back to 27, he took a peek between the shade and the edge of the window closest to him.

A good-looking guinea about thirty or so sat profile to him at the dinner table, eating something out of a bowl he held in his hand, talking to someone out of sight in what must be the kitchen. The guy's sleeveless undershirt let Katz see his biceps and the anchor tattoo decorating his shoulder. Could be trouble, he thought, but he'd decked bigger guys. He jogged up the two steps of the little open stoop and rapped his knuckles on the door, rat-a-tat-tat.

He pictured Formaroli pushing back the chair and striding across the little living room. He didn't think Gino was the kind of guy who'd peek through the window to see who it was and he was right. Formaroli threw the door open and looked down at him with what Sam took to be a little hostility.

"Yeah?"

"Are you Mr. Gino Formaroli?"

"Who are you?"

"I'm Sam Katz. Dunham's asked me to come see you."

"Oh yeah? The fuck they want?"

"You owe them ten dollars and thirty-five cents for an item you charged."

"Gino, who is it?" a voice blared from the back.

"No one. Stay there," he called back, then asked Katz "What kind of item?"

"Lady's jewelry. That's all I know."

A plump but pretty woman, thick black hair matted to her forehead, came into Sam's view, leaning out from the kitchen. Gino caught Sam's look over his shoulder and turned around to face her.

5

"Loretta! Get back in there. I got it, okay?"

Loretta lingered just a second, then disappeared back around the corner.

"Let's go outside," Gino said.

Sam backed down to the sidewalk to let him out the door, then watched Gino close it and point up the block towards Roebling. They walked side by side without saying a word till they got to the corner. Gino pulled an open pack of L&M's from his pants pocket, slid one out, and fired it up with a lighter. He took a deep drag, looked down each street, then tilted his head back to shoot a stream of smoke into the sky. Sam waited for him.

"I know what it is," Gino finally said. "It's a necklace."

"Okay," Sam said. "I hope your wife's enjoying it."

"My wife don't know I bought it."

This was not a new story to Sam.

"Makes no difference to me, Mr. Formaroli," he said. "I'm just here for the money."

Gino sucked down another long drag and swallowed it.

"It was, what d'you call it, a spur of the moment thing. Thought it would buy me a little something. *Capisce*?"

Sam capisced. This is how they live, he thought, but said nothing.

"How much I owe?" Gino asked.

"Ten dollars and thirty-five cents. No interest if you pay it all today."

"Shit, man, I ain't got ten dollars and thirty-five cents on me. Tomorrow's payday. Come back then, I'll have it all for you, no sweat."

"I'm here now, Mr. Formaroli. I need something to show Dunham's."

6

Gino looked him up and down, threw his cigarette down, and ground it into the sidewalk with the toe of his black loafer.

"And what if I ain't got it?"

Sam stepped closer to him, where he could get a sharp shot in but Gino couldn't.

"Mr. Formaroli, I only want you to give me a little something to take back to Dunham's. You do that, you can just make up a nice little story to tell your wife. You want to tell her why that guy beat the shit out of you? That's your choice."

He was close enough to Gino to see the sweat shine off his forehead. Gino kept his eyes on Sam's, then backed up a step and reached into his back pocket for his wallet. He looked into the billfold.

"I only got three bucks on me."

"I don't want to wipe you out," Sam said. "I'll take two."

Gino started to protest but decided not to push it. He pulled two wrinkled one-dollar bills out and handed them to Sam. Sam folded them up and tucked them into his right suit pocket. He pulled the notebook paper from his left pocket, unfolded it, unclipped a pen from the same pocket, and took his time writing "$2.00 March 27" next to Gino's name.

"This is just between you and me, right?" Gino asked.

"I'll be back for the rest tomorrow. Then you'll never see me again," Sam said.

I pray to Christ, Gino thought, but he said "You miserable fucking kike shylock bastard."

Sam had heard that before too. He pushed his index finger hard into Gino's chest and let it stay there till he saw the sweat pop out again, then said "See you tomorrow."

He turned to the right down Roebling, ears pricked to hear Gino rush him from behind. But he heard nothing and let his mind wander to Fanny and Jake and home.

He turned down the alley where he left the car, a '54 plum-colored Ford, down near the Hudson end. He couldn't see it in the dark but figured it had to be down there somewhere behind the car with the big fins and in front of one of those new Mercury Montereys, all black and sleek. He promised himself that would be his next car, still a Ford but with a little more pizzazz. He took it in as he got closer until he heard feet pounding up the pavement his way and looked up to see the tall colored kid he saw before running towards him with an even taller white kid, a teenager in a black jacket, close behind and gaining. Sam heard him yell, "You better run, nigger boy! Run, boy!"

Behind them, Sam saw another white kid pinning the other colored kid against the car in front of his. The glint of a street light let him make out two bikes laying cockeyed on the sidewalk at Hudson. The boy on the run shot past him, the bigger kid maybe ten yards behind.

Sam stepped into his path and held up a hand.

"Stop it! Let him go!"

The kid ran wide to get around him. Sam took a step to his right and lowered a shoulder into his rib cage, lifting him off his feet and bouncing him off a chain link fence at the side of the alley. Sam turned around to see the colored boy looking back at him, frozen in his tracks.

"Go! Go!" Sam yelled at him and waved him away, but the boy didn't move.

"My bike!" he said, pointing back down the alley.

The guy who bounced off the fence rolled to his knees and glared up at Sam.

"The fuck was that, man?"

"Let them go," Sam said. "Let them get their bikes and go."

"Ray, what's going on down there?" the other white kid yelled.

"Nothin', Frankie. Just some asshole lookin' for a beatin'." He pushed himself up off the ground and sprang at Sam all in one motion. Sam clipped him on the left cheek with a short right and put him back down. He didn't hurry to his feet this time.

Sam looked back at the kid behind him and motioned him to come back down. The kid kept his eyes on Ray the whole way back until Sam threw an arm around his shoulders and guided him back up the alley.

Frankie saw them coming but he didn't see Ray.

"Ray, man, what's going on?" he called out.

"Turn little fat Sambo loose!" he heard.

When they got to his car, Sam let go of the tall kid and motioned him to stay there. Frankie held the other kid by his arms, pushed against the driver's side of the car with the fins. When Sam moved towards them, he saw it was a De Soto with New York plates, two-tone, red over white. He stopped at the rear bumper.

"Listen to your friend," he said. "Let him go."

"Who are you, man, the Lone Fucking Ranger?" Frankie said, but he let him go, holding his hands up high. Sam turned back to the tall boy and motioned him towards the bikes. The kid ran past Frankie, and his friend ran after him. They picked up their bikes and took off up Hudson to the right.

Sam turned back to his car, but he never made it all the way around. He took Ray's uppercut full on the chin and staggered back towards the De Soto. When he lost consciousness, he fell to the ground, his fall broken only by the driver's side fin piercing his temple. Blood gushed out over his suit, splashing onto the alley. He slid down the side of the car, leaving a thick red smear all the way down the wheel well before pitching face down to the ground.

Frankie looked down at Sam, then at Ray hovering over him, then back at the still body, waiting to see if it moved. It didn't.

"Jesus, man! Is he dead?" Frankie said.

"The fuck's it look like, man?" Ray said.

He threw open the back door, then rolled Sam on to his back.

"Get his legs, quick!"

"That's gonna fuck up the upholstery, man!" Frankie said, "My father'll fuckin' kill me!"

"Fuck your upholstery! Get his legs, now!"

"Hold on! Hold on!"

Frankie fumbled in his pocket for the keys. He rattled the trunk key into the hole and popped it open. Ray got his arms under Sam's and lifted. Frankie picked up him by the ankles and wheeled him around to his left so Ray could get between the cars and roll Sam in head first. They stuffed the rest of him in the trunk and Frankie slammed it shut. Ray ran around to the passenger side and Frankie scrambled to the driver's side, jumping over the puddle of blood still widening on the concrete.

"Go, go, go!" Ray said but Frankie didn't need to be told. He lurched it forward the ten yards to Hudson, then slammed on the brakes. He saw the colored kids wheeling away from him up the sidewalk.

"Which way, man?"

Ray waved to the left.

"It's one-way, that way! Go, go, go!"

Frankie patched out to the left.

"Now where?" he asked.

"Shut the fuck up a second!" Ray said. "Let me think!"

There was way too much to think about but getting rid of the dead bastard in the trunk was first and foremost. His brother Dom would know how but he wasn't going to take the time to call him. Plus, the less people that knew about this, the better.

"There's a light up there," he heard Frankie say. "Where should I go?"

And on top of everything, he had to do it all himself. His harebrained cousin from the Bronx didn't even know where the hell he was. He thought. That was South Clinton. Right would take them downtown, left to spook town. Straight went to the brewery, and the Delaware.

"Straight, man, straight!" Ray yelled. Frankie floored it through just as the light turned red.

"Now where, now where?"

Ray was going to fucking kill him.

"Stop asking!" he yelled. "I'm gonna tell you, just shut up! Keep going through the next light! And slow down! We don't need cops pulling us over."

Frankie took his foot off the gas for a second but put it right back down hard to make sure he made the light at South Broad.

"All right," Ray said "you're gonna make a right on Cass, then a left on Canal."

Frankie got the green at Cass. He was dying to ask how far it was to Canal but he kept his mouth shut till he got right up on the next light and it turned yellow. He didn't see a sign for Canal so he floored it.

"Left, you dumb bastard, left!" Ray screamed.

Frankie banked the DeSoto wide into the turn and pumped the brakes hard to keep it on the road.

"It said 129!" he yelled over the squealing.

11

"129, Canal, same difference. Just keep going till I tell you to turn! One more right and we're there."

"There where?" Frankie asked. "Where we goin'?"

"The brewery," Ray said.

"The brewery where you work?"

"No, some other fuckin' brewery."

"What if someone's there? What if they recognize you?"

"No one's there, man, trust me. Just drive."

At the stop sign at Lamberton, Ray pointed to a gravel parking lot across the street next to a brick building with "Home of Champale" painted on the wall in big flowing white letters. Two long trailers sat at the loading dock to the right.

"Go across," Ray said.

Frankie crossed Lamberton and crunched slowly across the gravel. He looked past the lot and saw a field of grass running down to a bunch of tall trees hiding whatever was behind them.

"Pull over here," Ray said. Frankie saw him jerk his thumb to an open space between the trailers, then eased into the space until he was right against the wall under the dock. He pried his hands off the steering wheel and turned the ignition off.

"Wait here," Ray said and jumped out of the passenger's side.

Frankie looked in the mirror to see him run past the back of the car, then disappear. He heard Ray's feet run across the gravel then he didn't hear anything. That was when he realized his Goddamn cousin just left him alone here with a dead body in his trunk. He smacked the steering wheel with both hands. Tears leaped to his eyes and he made a noise he never remembered making before, a short sharp whine like he had a cat trapped in his throat. That damn Ray left him sitting here to take the rap, just like that! Probably planned it the whole time. He didn't even know his way out of this shithole of a city. Just his luck, a cop would pull him over and his ass would be grass.

In the trunk, Sam felt his hand sticking to the side of his head. It took some effort to open his eyes but it was just as dark as when they were closed. He closed them again.

Ray threw his head back and pounded his fists on his forehead. God damn but he was tired of this bullshit! If he got out of Jersey, he was going back to the Bronx, packing his bags, and heading to Florida, where he knew no one and no one knew him. Get a job at one of the race tracks, lay out in the sun, start all over. This was a sign, sure as hell. He almost shit his pants when Ray rapped his knuckles on the window.

"Let's go!" he said. "Let's get him out of here."

Frankie followed Ray to the back of the car and unlocked the trunk again. Sam had moved a little from where they left him. Ray rolled him on to his back, slid his arms under his armpits, and lifted his shoulders onto the edge of the trunk.

"Grab his feet," Ray said. Frankie pulled Sam's legs towards him and slid his hands down to his ankles. "Now lift him," Ray said. They lifted him up and out of the trunk.

"He's heavy," Frankie said.

"No shit," Ray said and tilted his head towards the trees. "This way."

Frankie let his cousin take the lead, backing his way to wherever they were going. When they got to the edge of the trees, he said "Ray, I gotta stop a second. He's killing me." Before Ray could say anything, he dropped Sam's feet and wiped the sweat from his face. Ray muttered something and let the rest of Sam fall to the ground. He stared at Frankie but said nothing.

"Ray, gimme a break. How much further we gotta carry him?"

"We'd a been there already if you hadn't stopped. You ready now?"

Frankie took a deep breath. He looked over Ray's shoulder and between the trees.

"What's back there, man?"

"A river. And a boat. You ready?"

He lifted and Frankie lifted and they waddled their way through the trees and off to the left through thick grass, then down a hill to the foot of a short dock at the edge of the water. A rowboat bobbed on the edge of the water just in front of them. Its metal hull smacked against a pillar, then drifted back onto the mud.

The chill air dried the sweat on Frankie's brow and made him shudder. He saw Ray squint into the woods.

"We need something heavy," Ray said. "You got anything in the car?"

"I got a spare battery in the trunk."

"That'll do," Ray said. "Go get it."

Frankie scrambled up the hill and thought: This is my chance. Start the car, back out, and go before Ray even knows it. Screw the Bronx, I'll go straight to Florida, with the flamingos and all that sun. But by the time he got to the trunk, he knew Ray would rat him out, pin the whole thing on him, that Goddamned weasel, so he popped the trunk.

He reached back for the Mopar battery that set him back eight forty-five. Eight and a half bucks, for what? An anchor? He lugged it back to the dock, cursing Ray every step.

"Perfect," Ray said when he dropped it at his feet. "Let's get him down there." They knew their positions by now and carried Sam around the far side of the rowboat.

14

"On three," Ray said and swung Sam's hefty body away from the boat. Frankie caught his rhythm.

"One, two, three," Ray said and on the last beat they pitched Sam into the boat. His left shoulder caught the edge and he fell back towards them until Ray shoved him back in. Sam's head struck a seat and stayed there. Ray reached back for an oar on the ground and handed it to Frankie.

"Put it in the other side," he said.

"Where?" Frankie said.

"What do you mean where? There's like a peg that goes into a hole over there. Look," he said, putting the other oar's peg into the hole on his side, "like this."

"Since when do you know anything about boats?" Frankie asked as he made his way around.

"Since I started borrowing this one at lunch and knocking down a few cold ones where the foreman can't see me."

Frankie found the hole on his side. By the time he got the thing into it, Ray was back in the boat with the battery. He put it in the back, then turned to see Frankie climbing in the boat.

"No, no, man, get back out. You got to push us off here."

Frankie got out and around to the back. He leaned into it and got the boat off the shore, then jumped back in and scrambled onto the rear seat, his feet squishing in his shoes.

Ray pulled on the rope hooked to the front to draw them towards the dock. He dug a little switchblade out of his pocket, sliced the rope from the boat, then rammed an oar into the side of the dock and pushed them away, out into the river. He kicked Sam's head off the seat to make some room, sat down, and started rowing. Frankie turned to see the land move away from them.

15

"Frankie, Frankie, the battery! Tie it to his Goddamn ankles. C'm'on, man, go!"

Frankie pushed Sam's legs together and wrapped the rope around his ankles three times. He tucked one end between his ankles and pulled the rope out and around the wrap he made another three times. He had about ten feet left, so he pulled it around the battery three times one way, then three times the other before making some kind of knot he thought would hold it all together. It's only gotta last a couple seconds, he told himself.

Ray rowed hard, sending sprays of water all over Sam and Frankie.

Sam's eyes popped open. He stared at the floor of the boat but saw nothing. He felt wet but didn't know why or where he was. He heard yelling but didn't understand a word.

Once they cleared the trees, Frankie looked down the river. He saw a bridge maybe a mile or so away. Big capital letters on its side spelled out "Trenton Makes, The World Takes." The river pulled them that way, faster than it looked from the shore. He picked a bad time to remember he didn't swim so good.

"How far we going?" he shouted to Ray.

That's a good question, Ray thought. Before he got in the boat, he was going to go out to the middle and dump the fucker where no one would ever find him. But he was busting his hump and they'd only gone maybe fifty yards. There was no way he was going to make it to the middle. He tucked one of the oars inside the boat then dipped the other one blade first into the water. He pushed it down till the whole thing was under and wiggled it around as best he could. He didn't feel bottom. Far enough. He pulled the oar up and threw it on the other one.

"Right here. Let's go!"

16

Go where? Go how? Frankie asked himself. The boat was swaying and rocking like crazy. How were they going to get this lump over the edge without going in themselves?

"How we supposed to do this, man?"

"Put the battery over here," Ray yelled, pointing to the space between the guy's body and the other side of the river. Frankie pushed it as far over there as he could without getting off the seat. The boat tipped from the extra weight and Frankie grabbed the edge of the boat again. He heard Ray yell, "No, no, over there!"

Frankie looked up to see him pointing to the other side of the boat. He shimmied over and grabbed that side of the boat with both hands, then moved one knee at a time until he was all the way over. He looked back over his shoulder at Ray who had slid down his seat the other way.

"All right," Ray said. "Now turn your ass around."

Frankie grabbed the edge of his seat, spun himself on his knees, crawled back as far as he could, then turned his knees one at a time to face down the river, the guy practically under him, Ray just past the guy. The boat looked like it was sitting on the river like a bathtub but every little lurch sent him grabbing for something, anything to hold on to.

"Look at me, Frankie, look at me!" Ray said.

Frankie looked at him.

"This is the way we're going to do it. I'm going to drop the battery over first, okay? You're going to lean your ass back against that side there as far as you can, okay? Because the boat's going to tip the other way, you got it?"

Frankie nodded.

"Soon as that thing goes over, I'm going to pull his head and shoulders up over the edge

17

-- you stay where you are, right? Keep us balanced, okay? Then we're both going to get our legs under him and kick him up and over, flip him over the edge. You got it?"

Frankie wasn't sure he got it but nodded anyway. Just get it over with, man, his only thought.

Ray leaned forward, grabbed the battery with two hands, and pulled it to his chest.

"Fucker's heavy," he said. No shit, Frankie thought.

Ray swung the battery to his left, then let it sail out to the right. It cleared the edge and pulled Sam's legs that way too. That made Ray reconsider.

"Okay, I'll get his legs over, then we'll push him from the top. Be easier."

He leaned over Sam's body and yanked and yanked until he finally got his ankles up and over the side of the boat. The pull of the rope arched his feet down and pushed his hips up, like he was humping someone, Frankie thought.

"Now, push, push, push!" They leaned into and under Sam's shoulders till they got the small of his back up on the edge.

"Get back to the other side!" Ray said and pushed hard on Sam's shoulders to send him over.

Sam felt himself fall. His arms stabbed out to grab onto something. His right hand found it but it didn't stop him from going over, under, and down, dragging Ray with him.

Ray clawed at the hand wrapped around his wrist but it was locked on tight. With the weight of a dead man and the Mopar pulling him down, his last thought was "Fucking niggers!".

Frankie pitched into the river. He flipped onto his back to keep his head out of the water and watched the inside of the boat slam down around him like a coffin lid. He grabbed Ray's seat with both hands, his frantic breathing

18

echoing off the inside of the hull. When he got himself under control, he looked down into the water, searching for any sign of Ray but all he saw was dark.

He moved his hands one at a time till they both clutched the edge of the seat nearest one side. He took a deep breath and bobbed under. He pulled his hands off the seat one at a time and came up outside clinging to the boat, one hand on an oarlock, one hand on the edge. He drank in the air till he couldn't take in any more.

He looked over his shoulder. The bridge with the sign was coming closer to him, but there was another bridge even closer. The boat headed for a cut of land stabbing out from the Jersey side just in front of it. He knew he needed to get back to the car and get the hell out of here but he wondered, if he kicked the boat way out into the middle, how long it would take the river to pull him to Florida.

April 4, 1968

1

When Brenda Queen felt that cobra rise to squeeze her again, she pitched towards the mirror and clawed at the edge of the sink to brace herself. The beast pushed its way between every rib, grabbed her heart, slithered up her neck, and burst into her head, hugging her brain in its sweet, sweet grip.

The speaker up in the corner rasped out the Velvelettes covering "Heat Wave". She closed her eyes and cooed the tune to herself, hanging there, waiting for the jolt to end, then praying for just one more.

From her perch on the toilet down to the left, Leelee kept her eyes fixed on Brenda's reflection, never missing a beat stroking her silky brown wig. She watched her face crinkle and her smile twist, just like the ladies in the church when they got what they called the raptures. Brenda was the only lady she ever saw get them in the bathroom.

When the snake finally released her, Brenda slowly opened her eyes and tried to focus on the face looking back at her. Even in the hard light glaring off that crappy mirror, she looked pretty damn good for forty-three, even the thirty-five that only her brothers knew was a lie. Creamy cocoa skin, still taut over the cheekbones, green eyes that peered out from under a smooth forehead, no lines, no wattles, no gray flecking those tight coils.

That mirror said everything that needed to be said about that tightwad bastard Em Crowe. The first time she came through the Howard, three years ago now, there was just a hole and a spider crack down the other end. The joke was that Big Flo Ballard of the Supremes put it there when she saw what she really looked like and threw a shoe at it.

But it was no joke now. Sometime before her next time through, the top of the whole left side cracked and fell, leaving a jagged line of loose glass running down diagonal to just in front of her. She still had to brush new little flecks off the counter before every show, four times a day, five on Saturday. Now the only place to get a good look at yourself was all the way down by the window which had to stay open all the time to get some air in which was why she was standing there getting wet when the rain started coming through. Broken mirror's bad luck all right, but she swore it'd be worse for that cheap nappy-headed buzzard Em Crowe than it would ever be for her.

She shot Leelee a quick look in the mirror and wiggled her fingers at the window. Leelee sat the wig on the rack on the floor, stood up, wedged the brush handle into the top of her too tight black skirt, and crossed behind Brenda to the window.

Brenda watched her go. That poor sad simple child, she thought, just as thick in the middle and dumpy in the butt as the last time she and the Jacks came through, but thicker on the top now too. Her sweet face and full brown eyes were pretty, but even that was a curse because they'd just bring her into harm's way, a slow, fat target for any nigger looking to score a piece of ass. From the back, raggedy strands stuck out every which way from that natural pile all around her head.

Brenda turned to see Leelee reach out and pull the window down, then cross back to clump down on the toilet seat lid and pick up her wig again. Brenda winced watching her try to jerk the brush free from her pants.

"Leelee, honey, stand up. It'll be easier."

Leelee stood back up, slid the brush out, sat back down, and set to stroking again.

Brenda heard some tinny applause filter through the box. Not much of a crowd, she thought, even for a Thursday afternoon. She wiped a streak of something off the glass in

22

front of her and turned the hot faucet on high to get whatever it was off her hand.

"Leelee, when is your uncle going to take care of this place, huh?"

Leelee didn't know the answer to that, so she just sat there and kept brushing, happy to hear Brenda answer it herself.

"Never, that's when! Not like this at the Apollo, I'll tell you that. Got a real dressing room there, little table to put your things on, little bench to park your butt, pretty mirrors with lights all around. Makes you feel like bein' a star, puttin' on a show! This," she swung her arm, "makes you feel like takin' a shit!"

Leelee kept her head down and brushed. She heard this from Brenda before, every time before in fact.

"You know that wall down there in the green room where everybody leaves a little message, signs their names?"

Leelee knew the wall she was talking about. The room was gray, though, not green, but she didn't think this was a good time to say that.

"Well, that's what I'm going to write on it," Brenda went on, scribbling in the air, "'This place makes me feel like takin' a shit! Brenda Queen'. Serve that old bastard right. If I ever – *ever* – say I'm going to play the Howard Theatre again, I want someone to stand up and shoot me, kill me dead!"

She pitched forward again, stabbing her hands at the counter to keep from falling into the sink. She knew good and well this was the last squeeze so she milked it right to the end. This shit was Maxwell Horse, baby. Good to the last drop.

When she opened her eyes this time, it was Leelee's reflection she saw. She turned and leaned back against the sink, watching her sit on the crapper, head down, stroking and stroking.

"Leelee, honey, you brushed it enough. Put it down now and get me my dress."

Leelee put the wig on the rack, stood up, tucked the brush in her skirt, and walked over to where Brenda's sparkly green and purple dress hung on the door. She brought it to Brenda who lowered it over her head and shimmied herself into it in all in one motion. Brenda reached over for her black cotton cap, squeezed it on to her head and patted it into place. She folded over two pieces of masking tape and offered them to Leelee on the tips of her fingers. Leelee took them one at a time and put them just where Brenda pointed on the cap. Then she went back to the stall, picked up the wig, and walked it back to Brenda, holding it high up in front of her like the lady did with the crown for the other Queen in that movie she saw.

Brenda dipped her head and let Leelee pull the wig down over it, feeling her breasts push against her own. Brenda turned to the mirror and tugged the wig into place, then met Leelee's eyes in the mirror.

"Leelee," she asked, "how old are you now?"

"Twelve," Leelee said.

"Twelve? My lord, you look like you could be fifteen or sixteen with them --" but she let the rest of it die on her tongue. She felt so sorry for this child who had no idea what was coming her way, wouldn't have an idea when it got to her. Lord knows her Uncle Em wouldn't tell her.

"Leelee honey, I was a girl just like you not too long ago and I wish somebody'd told me what I'm going to tell you now. Child, look at me."

Leelee lifted her head and saw Brenda's reflection point a shaking finger at her.

"Here it is: Do not trust a man. Do *not* trust a man. *Ever*. Do you hear me?"

"Yes, ma'am."

"You trust only yourself because nobody else is going to look out for you. You're a woman now, Leelee -- yes you are -- and you've got to protect yourself and think of yourself and what's good for you, first and only, because a man isn't going to do that, no matter what he says. Are you following me?"

Leelee saw tears in Brenda's eyes, little streams of them running down her cheeks.

Brenda tried to keep the faces from crowding her mind, but she didn't have to see them. They ate at her heart and soul every day.

"I have been a sinner, Leelee. I have sinned. I ain't made no idols and I ain't killed no one – yet -- but everything else that's unholy, child, I done it and I'm sorry but if I have to, I would do it again, every one of 'em, every time. I have committed adultery, I have coveted my neighbor's house, I have borne false witness, I have stolen. Don't drop your head down, girl. You look at me and you listen. You learn from me, okay?"

Leelee picked up her head. Brenda's eyes jumped right out at her.

"I didn't want to do it, Leelee. As Jesus Christ is my witness, I never meant to do any of it. But, child, a man will lie and cheat and build you up and rip you down and use you and abuse you and make you think you're the queen of the world, then shit on you in a heartbeat."

"I don't know any men," Leelee said.

"You will though, girl, and they will come lookin' for you, huntin' for you in real short order 'cause you got what they want already. I'm trying to prepare you, to warn you, for your own good. Men are looking for what's between

25

your legs and they will do anything to get there. They will rob you blind, give you things you don't want or need but make you crave for . . ."

She heard the Velvelettes start "Needle In A Haystack" below them. Their finale. Her cue.

She turned back to the mirror and leaned on the counter one more time to steel herself. When she was ready, she closed her right eye to lay a false eyelash on it. She reached for the other lash and caught a glimpse of Leelee, her head down, her eyes watery. Holding her hands in front of her, she seemed smaller now. It stabbed Brenda, hurt her heart that she caused that sad girl such pain. She turned back to her.

"Leelee," she said softly and repeated it before Leelee raised her eyes to look at her. Brenda cocked her head and smiled at her.

"I'm sorry to lay all my wicked secrets on you, child, okay? Do you forgive me?"

Leelee cast her eyes back down and nodded slowly. Brenda turned back to the mirror with her left lash on her finger.

"Now you tell me all yours, serve me right."

When she thought she heard Leelee mumble something, she turned back.

"Honey, what did you say?"

Leelee kept her eyes on the ground, then said it again, just loud enough to not make Brenda ask her again.

"I only know one," she said.

2

Lisa told him about Reverend King just as he walked in the door.

"Martin Luther King's been shot! He's dead! Jake, my God!"

Floyd told him about Brenda Queen when he picked up the phone.

"Looks like they got all the nigger royalty tonight, Ikey."

"What?"

"King and Queen. Your girl Brenda, the singer? At the Howard, tonight."

"How? What happened?"

"I'll fill you in at headquarters. Get movin'."

Lisa was frozen, staring at the television. Katz watched King in a march somewhere. He wanted to stay, learn the whole story, comfort his wife. She kept her eyes on the box, tears streaming down her cheeks.

"I gotta go," he said.

He watched her watch the television, then went out the door. There was nothing else to say.

Bacon bits spewing from a tub of tapioca. The image popped into Katz' head the first time he heard that accent spring out of Floyd Krebs' big round hairless face and stuck there forever. His mother met Floyd once on a visit, for five minutes. The door no sooner shut behind him than she pronounced him "the most *goyische* thing I ever saw."

Floyd hung the Ikey on him the day they were paired up.

"Jake Katz? What kind of name is that?" was the first thing out of his mouth. In Philly, everyone knew what kind of name it was but maybe where Floyd was from -- Philippi, West Virginia it turned out -- nobody did. So Katz could've given him the benefit of the doubt.

He didn't.

"Jake? You never met anyone named Jake?"

"I know guys named Jake, wiseass. I mean Katz. Where your people from?"

"Philadelphia. It's a city. In Pennsylvania. That's a state."

"Don't fuck with me, Katz. What are you, a Jew?"

"I am a Jew, Floyd. And how about you? You a Jew too?"

Floyd cut him a look, then shook his head.

"Ikey the Kikey they stick me with. Fuck me."

Katz considered his options. First day on a job he needed to make the money he needed to start law school at GW next fall. He could kiss it all goodbye before he even got started or he could suck it up and deal with it. He figured he could deal with anything for nine months, even Floyd.

"No problem," he said. "Fuck you."

Floyd would have to deal with him too.

Whoever drove got to choose the radio station. When they rode at night, Floyd pushed up WWVA from Wheeling, the "home of that fine country music, folks". Days he settled for whatever pop station played a song Katz couldn't stand. Night or day, Katz picked WOL, the home of Nighthawk Bob Terry and great R&B. Neither one of them ever said it out loud but a snap of Floyd's fingers, Katz's hum of a tune brought them closer together as the weeks rolled on.

The turning point came one muggy August morning just before dawn when they were cruising back to the station down 9th St. Soulfinger Fred Correy was pulling his own midnight shift on WOL. He loved James Brown's "I Can't Stand Myself" so much that he played it at least once an hour, often enough that both of them knew every one of James' grunts and inflections by heart. When it came on this time, Floyd rolled down his window so he could bang his hand on the roof, off-time, of course. It didn't stop him though, he was in his groove.

"Good Gawd!" he honked along with James, "Good Gawd!"

James moved on but Floyd kept the "Good Gawds!" coming with a series of moves that would have gotten him pummeled at the Howard, or maybe anywhere. He flapped his arms like a chicken, he bounced off his seat, he screamed his "Good Gawd!s" at pedestrians who could only stare back in wonder at the crazy white cop rolling past. Katz broke out laughing and begged him to stop but he wouldn't even when they pulled into the station, both of them crying, dying with laughter.

Katz came to trust Floyd enough to invite him to join his old GW buddies for beers and burgers after work. They always met at either Casino Royale or Rand's, the two most popular strip joints on 14th St. Living with Lisa had dimmed Katz's fascination with the random naked breast but the rest

29

of the crew enjoyed them as much as ever so he knew better than to suggest anywhere else. Tonight it was Rand's.

Most of them had stayed in town after graduation. Mike Weiss, single but shacked up and as good as married to his girlfriend Anne, was at GW Law, a few worked on the Hill, others just hung around finding new ways to avoid the draft. Floyd was fascinated by all of them, but none more than fat Andy Scheingold, another Jew who loved soul music as much as Katz and ate as much as he could as often as he could to stay over 242 pounds, the weight a 5-8 guy had to be to be too fat for Nam.

Scheingold loved to tell the story about the time he and Katz cut class to see Brenda Queen and the Jacks at the Howard, and Floyd loved to hear it, every time.

"So they do four shows a day, and we decide to duck out to see a 2 o'clock show on whatever it was, a Tuesday or something, " he said, burger juice trickling through his scraggly beard.

"It was a buck fifty to go to a matinee," Katz said, "to see her and a whole revue."

"And you had that student discount card," Floyd reminded them.

"Right," Scheingold said. "So it was 75 cents to see the whole show. We go in there and it's the two of us and a drunk sleeping it off in the back row. We figure they'll never put the show on for just two white guys and a drunk, but, lo and behold, 2 o'clock sharp, the lights go down, the curtain pulls back, and there they go, the whole show. I don't remember who else was on the bill -- "

"Linda Jones was one, I remember her," Katz said.

"Right," Scheingold said. "'Hypno-ti-i-ized.' Anyhow, finally, here comes Brenda Queen and the Jacks and they do like six or seven songs, just for us. It was incredible."

"And the sax player, don't forget the sax player," Floyd said.

Katz picked up the story while Scheingold pounded down a fistful of fries.

"Right. She was doing a version of 'Respect' and she was supposed to sing two verses, then the guy was supposed to do his sax solo. Well, she does the first verse and starts singing 'I ain't gonna do you no wrong' but all of a sudden he stands up and blasts his solo all over her. She shoots him a look but waits for him to finish, then ends the song like nothing happened. So the show ends, we give her a standing O, then start to head out."

"But," Scheingold said, "all of a sudden, the theatre goes dark again, a movie screen drops down, and they start showing this grade Z science fiction movie. Katz looks at his watch and says 'It's 3:15. The next show is at 4:30.' I say 'I got nowhere to go' so we sit down and watch this ridiculous movie, and then the next show starts and we're still the only people in the theater, us and the drunk, still there, still sleeping. Two shows, 75 cents, just for us."

"But here's the best part," Katz said. "The sax player? From the first show? Gone. Fired on the spot."

"Because he fucked up," Floyd said.

"In front of just two people," Scheingold said.

"And the drunk," Floyd said.

"And the drunk," Katz said. "That's why you have to give them respect, Floyd. Totally professional operation there, no matter who was watching or how many. It's still unbelievable to me, and I was there."

"'R-E-S-P-E-C-T'," Scheingold gargled through his beer.

"'Find out what you mean to me'," Floyd tried to sing.

"'Sock it to me, sock it to me, sock it to me, sock it to me'," they all sang.

4

Katz and Lisa lived on 26th Street in the same apartment he had at GW, with an unparalleled view of a ramp off the Whitehurst Freeway that ground to a halt in the grass right across the street. Driving to headquarters on Indiana, everything seemed the same as it did a few hours ago when he rolled out to take some statements about last night's brawl at Casino Royale, except the rain was picking up. He rolled the window halfway down anyhow just to let some air in. He loved his big black '59 Mercury Monterey but he vowed again that his next car had to have AC. Even in April, the mugginess was killing him.

HQ was wall to wall noise. On the way to the briefing room, he could only catch snippets of what was going on up 14th St. Floyd summed it up for him.

"Fuckin' niggers are goin' apeshit."

"What's that mean, exactly?" Katz asked.

"Settin' fires, breakin' windows, stealin' everything that ain't nailed down."

Floyd's pal Bailey poked his feral face between them.

"Shit keeps up, Martin Luther Coon's going to have some company real soon, I guaran-fuckin-tee you."

Katz heard Sgt. Jarvie on the bullhorn but he couldn't make out a word. They made their way to the edge of the crowd halfway down the hall from where Jarvie stood above them. He must have been on a chair but Katz could only see the lip of the horn and the sweat streaking down his gleaming head just behind it. Old as he was, he came to MPD just a few years ago after he quit his law firm downtown. The Chief thought his legal expertise might help rein in some of the more rambunctious boys in blue. Tonight would be a good test.

"Listen up, listen up! We've got a major situation developing out there. Tonight, everybody's CDU until we run out of riot gear." CDU was the Civil Disturbance Unit, created after last year's riots in Detroit and LA to make sure that if it ever came to it, DC's cops were prepared to handle the situation a hell of a lot better than theirs. But Katz never had a minute of riot training and he bet no one else in the room had either. So much for the best laid plans.

"When you come up here, grab a helmet, a baton, and a tear gas canister. Now here's the deal, listen close. You're there to keep the peace so you need to keep the stick swingin' and the gas to a minimum, okay? And no guns unless you fear for your life, that's the rule."

"Fuck that," Bailey muttered behind him and he had a lot of company. "Check this out."

Katz turned to see him slide a gloved hand into his left pants pocket and pull out the grip of a small black handgun.

"What's that?" Floyd asked.

"Drop gun, baby."

Floyd didn't get it. Neither did Katz. Bailey slid it back down.

"You need to use a gun," Bailey said, "you use it, then you drop it. No prints, no serial number, no problem."

"Where'd you get it?" Floyd asked.

"Hey, hey!" Jarvie boomed over the bitching. "The idea is to keep things in hand, not give anyone an excuse to go wild. No one wants DC to be another LA."

"Woolworth's, man," Bailey whispered, then laughed at them both. "Don't worry about it. No one'll ever trace it, guaran-fuckin'-teed."

They surged forward, Katz's nose pressed tight to Floyd's back.

34

"What a clusterfuck," he heard Bailey say right before an acrid smell filled the air and a cloud of white smoke ballooned its way past them along the low ceiling. Katz's eyes stung and wiping them only made it worse. Floyd spun back to him and buried his face in Katz's shirt. Curses filled the air.

"Jesus Christ!" Jarvie bellowed into the bullhorn. "Keep a grip on that shit!"

Hacking and wheezing their way to the front, they grabbed gas masks and strapped them on as quick as they could. Katz worked on Floyd's and Floyd returned the favor until they finally drew oxygen instead of sulfur. They gave each other the thumbs up, grabbed their batons and helmets, and made it to the street.

A sergeant pointed them to a squad car with two guys already in the front seat. They jumped in the back and the car took off. They made their way up Mass, around Thomas Circle and up 14th, lights blazing and sirens blaring. Up ahead and in the side view mirror, he could see other patrol cars and paddy wagons two and three abreast all the way up. At Swann, just above S, they made a left and slammed to a stop behind a bus unloading real CDU men. They fell in behind and marched onto 14th.

Deep inside the formation, it struck Katz that they must make a pretty intimidating sight, marching ten across, dark visors masking their faces, heavy oak batons at the ready. At least he hoped so.

His hope faded when they crossed T Street and he saw a mob of people, mostly Negroes, leaping in and out of broken store windows, racing in every direction. He saw flames rise from the darkness on both sides of the street. Who's intimidating who?, he thought.

The formation came to a halt just below U, then the cops in the front lines were suddenly coming his way.

"Fall back! Fall back!" he heard and he didn't wait to be told again. A Sergeant passed him, yelling into his walkie-talkie. "No way, without a shitload more men. There's way too many of 'em."

They regrouped below T and waited for reinforcements. In a few minutes, they turned around and headed back up with about three times the number of men they had the first time. Still not enough, not even close, Katz thought, but he made himself keep marching. The mob was bigger now too and paid them no mind, men and women, boys and girls darting into stores and coming out with suits and slacks slung over their shoulders, TV's, radios, and lamps piled in their arms. As long as the cops were happy to just stand there and watch, they were happy to give them the show.

Looking up 14th, Katz saw a double line of headlights and beacons cresting over the hill. The cavalry was on the way.

"OK, men, go get 'em," he heard. "Arrest anyone you see with shit in their hands, comin' in or out of anywhere, and run 'em back to the wagons. Move, move, move!"

There were so many targets, Katz didn't know where to run first. He saw two guys zip past him west on V, hangers full of clothes flapping behind them. He tapped Floyd on the shoulder and motioned him to follow him east on V. Almost at the end of the block, up on the right, he saw a steady stream of traffic racing in and out of a men's clothing store. Bailey ran past them both, flying through the open doorway, stick swinging wildly. Katz tackled the first guy ducking out of the way, pinned him to the sidewalk, and slapped the cuffs on him. Floyd pinned a girl, maybe a teenager, up against the frame of the smashed-in show window while another girl tried to pull him off, kicking and

36

flailing at his back. Katz jumped up to pull her off and wrestled her to the ground. He knelt on her back and watched the first perp careen down the street, hands cuffed behind him.

Bailey dragged a moaning man out of the doorway by the collar of his shirt. Blood smeared the concrete as he slid him towards Katz.

"Cuff this fucker. I'm going in for more."

By the time Katz got them both to their feet, Bailey was back out, empty handed this time.

"Fucking bunnies know how to run, I'll tell you that."

He heard a snort from across the street and spun around to see two Negro men, one maybe in his 20's, the other younger, leaning against a doorway, smiling at him.

"This is fucking funny to you?"

The smiles stayed frozen on their faces. Their hands stayed deep in their pockets.

Bailey strode across the street. Katz froze too, his eyes riveted on Bailey's left hand as it swung quickly past his pants pocket, then back again, twice, then three times. The older guy on the right stepped towards him, maybe to shield the younger one. It was hard to tell. Katz let out a breath only when Bailey reached out his left arm to grab him by the front of his shirt then winced when Bailey brought the club in his right hand down heavy across his collar bone. He crumpled to the ground. When his buddy bent down to check him out, Bailey crashed the baton down on his skull, sending him sprawling across the other. Bailey turned back to Katz and the commotion on the street. The crowd watching him took off in both directions. He crossed back to the store.

"What was that for?" Katz asked.

Bailey ignored him and pushed the girl Katz was holding back towards 14th.

The rest of the night was a blur to Katz. He remembered throwing his canister through the smashed-out display window at Belmont TV, tackling a man running out, and watching the set he was carrying fly into the street, smashing apart on impact. He remembered chasing men and women of all ages up and down alleys, some of them dropping their booty, some hanging on for dear life, and almost all of them getting away. He tripped over something sometime, spraining his ankle. He felt the pain every time he jogged up and down 14th St. to stand guard for one fire truck after another so their crews could work without getting pelted by stones or worse. That's why he was at the corner of Fairmont St. when the squad car rolled past, the bullhorn telling them they could all stand down when their relief came. He looked up and down the street. Except for the cops and the firemen, it was empty. He pushed his sleeve back to take a look at his watch. 7:45. Counting his time at Casino Royale, he figured he'd been on duty for 12 hours straight. It seemed like 12 days. He pushed himself up the bus steps and looked forward to heading home, lying in the tub, and catching up with Lisa about Memphis and Dr. King and Brenda Queen. Then he fell asleep.

5

He was still groggy coming off the bus -- until he heard someone say he was going to take a ride up 7ᵗʰ Street. The Howard was at 7ᵗʰ and T. He turned to see the someone was Deputy Chief Pine. He had never talked to a Captain before, much less a Chief, but he needed to go there, see what had happened, see if he could help. He felt he owed Brenda Queen that, if only for those two shows that afternoon. Pine told him to hop in the back.

Driving up 7ᵗʰ, he remembered his walk back down at midnight after seeing James Brown do a 10:00 Saturday show. He recalled every moment like it was only yesterday. He was mortified to remember it was only last year.

He and Scheingold had taken the bus up, getting off at New York Av, then transferring up 7ᵗʰ. He had three fifty with him, a quarter for the bus up and back and three bucks for the show, just what he paid to see The King of Soul the last time he was in town. He figured if he got held up waiting for the bus back after the show, they'd leave him alone if he had nothing in his wallet. Thinking about it now sent a shiver up his spine. Stupid was way too kind to describe it.

He had a chance to show a little smarts when he got to the box office and saw it was three and a quarter to get in this time. After cleverly deducing that if he bought the ticket, he'd have nothing left for the bus back, he asked Schein if he brought any extra money.

"I brought an extra quarter, just in case."

Another genius but still smarter than him.

"You're not gettin' on that bus without me, man."

"No, no, I won't leave you here, man, I swear."

Katz had serious doubts but still awash in idiocy and the prospect of seeing the greatest live show on earth, he bought the ticket anyway.

Scheingold stayed right on his tail as they pushed through the lobby and into the theater. Katz nodded at a pair of seats midway down one of the back aisles to the right. They sidled past a middle-aged couple and their young son and dropped quickly into the seats. They never had a minute of trouble at The Howard, but they didn't push their luck either.

Katz scanned the crowd for any white face other than Schein's and came up empty. Looking down his row, he saw the kid next to Schein gawking at him. He was maybe nine or ten with a broad round face and big eyes. He turned back to whisper to his mother. She looked Katz's way and smiled. Katz smiled back and when the kid turned back to him, still wide-eyed, he asked him "Everything okay?"

The kid said "You here for the show?"

Katz said "Guess so."

The kid leaned across Schein and flipped open his palm.

"Gimme some skin, man!" he shouted.

Katz laughed and slapped his hand. Schein did the same. The kid bounced back into his seat and his mother drew him to her.

"He's very excited," she told them.

"So are we," Scheingold said.

Red curtains hid the stage. Over the buzz of the crowd, Katz heard the plunk of an electric bass and the burp of a baritone sax. Then the place went dark and the crowd screamed, ready to pop. The curtains pulled back slowly, the stage bathed in darkness. Everyone jumped to their feet. Then, in an instant, lights flashed from up above and all around and the stage exploded in a whirl of sound and motion.

Katz roared, Scheingold threw his hands in the air, and everyone clapped hands to the hopping pulse of the music. James wasn't out there but the stage was filled from side to side, front to back.

Katz took the roll. At the left, the three Famous Flames moved as one, spinning, finger popping, shuffle stepping in time. Over at the right, three J.B.'s threw their hips left and right and their heads up and back, long manes of shiny black hair flying down, then flinging up. Behind them, the band swayed left and right, blowing trombones and saxes, crunching their axes, the rippling beat of the drums behind them and the chugging arms of the bandleader in front.

Off to the right, just behind the J.B.'s, two white-haired ladies flanked one white-haired gentleman, each of them clapping and bopping in time to the music. Katz looked for their violins and spotted them leaning against each seat. They were there for just one song: "This Is A Man's World," playing down that long intro, then plucking their strings against James' wails. The rest of the time, they just grooved like everyone else in the house.

The horn section took turns scatting over the beat until the house announcer, hidden in the wings, let everyone know the time had come.

"Ladies and gentlemen! Put your hands together for the hardest working man in show business!"

The horns blared in sync.

"The King of Soul!"

A higher blare.

"Soul Brother Number One!"

An insanely high note that made Katz wince.

"The One, The Only, James Brown!"

41

The roar filled the theatre to bursting. The crowd wanted its man and they got him, skidding out from the left wing on one foot, bending his leg like rubber as he somehow propelled himself to center stage. He grabbed the mike stand, pushed it towards the crowd, spun once, then twice, and grabbed it on the way back, pitching to his knees. He knelt there, sweating already, his shoulders heaving to the beat, waiting for the bass to lead the band into "Night Train," the hit that made him a star.

James hopped to his feet in one motion and slid in front of the Flames, falling in step with their bouncing rhythm, then showing them how it was really done .

"Miami, Florida!"

"Atlanta, Georgia!

"Raleigh, North Carolina!

"Washington, D.C.!"

The crowd roared louder than Katz thought possible.

When the train carried him home, James waved goodbye and left the stage to screams and cries from every corner of the house.

The kid next to Schein was frantic.

"Is he coming back, mommy! Is he? Is he?'

His mother hugged him near and patted his shoulder.

"Yes he is, darlin'. No need for worry. Just keep an eye out for him."

Bobby Bland fronted the Flames through "Stand By Me" and "The Dark End Of The Street" before the kid screamed and pointed at James when he popped back out to hear Miss Vicki Anderson beg him to "Think!", then disappeared again to leave everyone count down the minutes till he'd burst out to re-ignite them all.

And then there he was. "Cold Sweat". "Poppa's Got A Brand New Bag". "I Got You (I Feel Good)", and a special bonus for Katz, "Money Won't Change You". When

42

he heard what he called the "Hava Nagila" horns kick it off, he and Schein waited for their favorite line and screamed it together:

"If there's somebody that's once been hoit,

"Then you know how it feels to be treated – like doit!"

James took it down for "Man's World", up one more time for "Kansas City," then pulled everyone out of their seats for his killer finale.

"Please, please, please, please," James pleaded into the mike, his face ripped with anguish.

The Flames drove the point home. "Please, please, don't go," they crooned.

"I love you so!," James cried and hurtled to his knees.

The crowd screamed and swooned, then cheered when the bespectacled gentleman in the brown plaid suit rushed out from the wings and threw the red cape over James' shoulders. He wouldn't get up, couldn't get up, without his love even as the Flames pleaded with her, "Don't go." A beaten man, he finally made it to his feet. He trudged across the stage, bent over, a shadow of himself, too dispirited to go on, when suddenly, zeal somehow renewed, strength miraculously restored, he drummed his feet on the stage, threw off the cape, and strode back to the mike to beg her himself to stay.

The crowd ate it up, begging him to stay too. He stayed through one more, two more, three more breakdowns before he finally dragged himself into the dark and out of sight. He didn't stay gone long though, bounding back onto the stage, drenched in sweat, but still able to shimmy all the way across and back again, and toss his cufflinks to the crowd before disappearing for good to get himself ready to come back out and do it all over again a half an hour later.

Katz and Scheingold were drenched too, wiped out by what they had just seen, heard, and somehow lived through.

It was only when the house lights came up that Katz remembered he had a problem.

When they hit the sidewalk, he saw the line waiting for the midnight show. He started at the front and worked his way back.

"Hey, brother, you got a quarter to help me get home?" He cringed even now thinking about it. They all looked at him like he just landed from Mars, which maybe he did.

He looked at Scheingold, so pale he was practically transparent, wishing he was anywhere but here right now, wishing most of all he was on that bus just pulling up to the stop across the street. Today Katz knew that they could hop on that bus without paying a cent and the driver wouldn't give a good goddamn. But then? So naïve.

Katz went back to the entrance where a group of cops chatted among themselves.

"Hi," he interrupted. "Can one of you guys lend me a quarter to get a bus out of here?" This got nothing. "I don't want to make you have to come back later, you know, pick me up with a blotter." Nothing again. He turned to Scheingold.

"You remember what Sonny Hobson said?" Sonny Hobson was the premier soul deejay in Philly, where they both first fell in love with the music. Scheingold gulped and nodded.

"'Ain't nothin' to it but to do it'?"

Katz nodded. "It's time to do it."

So they walked to the corner at 7th and looked south towards New York, where all they'd have to contend with was drunk soldiers on leave. To get there, they'd have to make their way through ten of the blackest, roughest blocks

44

in the city, teeming with people and cars. They tried to stay out of the light and hugged as close to the walls as they could. When a crowd of brothers loomed ahead, they crossed the street and tried to disappear on the other side. More than once the safest place was on the yellow lines, walking double time between the four lanes of traffic roaring by. Neither of them said a word or even made a sound other than a sharp intake of breath when danger lay ahead. The walk seemed interminable until somehow, some way, they found themselves alone with the honky-tonk lights of New York Av just ahead.

Was that really him? Had he really been that pitifully innocent so little time ago? Chief Pine brought him back to the present.

"Here you go."

Katz saw they were at T.

"If you find anything interesting, you let the detectives know, okay?"

"Absolutely. Thanks."

He was relieved that the block looked the same as ever, nothing like the war zone he'd just left on 14th. He walked around the corner to the entrance on T. He tried the double doors and peeked through the glass. The lobby was empty. He knocked loudly and waited a minute, then walked around the corner to Wiltberger Street and tried a side door. Locked too. He came back around front and saw the door farthest from him just about to close. He sprinted to it and wedged a hand in just in time. He pulled it open and saw a short Negro with close cut gray hair and thick black-rimmed glasses turn to him.

"Good morning. I'm Jake Katz. I'm with MPD?"

"I can see that."

"Right. I just came by to see if I could find out what happened here last night, help with the investigation in any way."

"Detective came and went last night. Talk to him."

"I will, I definitely will. Do you remember his name?"

The other man shook his head and walked up an incline towards the theatre. At the top, he motioned for Katz to follow him. He did but he stopped at the top of the center aisle, taking it all in. It seemed so much smaller when it was empty. The red double curtains hung closed at the lip of the stage, brighter and glossier than the frayed red seats in front of him. There was plenty of trash in the aisles but not much noticeable damage. He'd pictured the same mob he saw on 14th St., tearing through the place, wreaking mayhem, ripping out the fixtures, leaving Brenda Queen and who knows how many others dead in their wake. He was relieved to be wrong.

He jogged down the aisle to catch up with the old man. He followed him past the orchestra pit and around the stage to the left, then down a narrow hallway with yellow paint peeling from both walls and a carpet that years of shoe leather had rendered a muddy brown.

The office sat at the end of the hall, windowless and barely wide enough for the desk that filled it.

Katz saw a dusty nameplate that read "Emmett Crowe General Manager."

"Are you Mr. Crowe?" Katz asked.

"Now who else would I be?" he said, rifling through the papers strewn across the desktop.

"I'm really honored to meet you. I come here a lot."

Crowe turned his head and gave him the once over.

"I thought I knew all the guys that work this place."

"No, I haven't worked here. I've been here for shows."

Crowe turned back to the desk.

"Oh, is that right? And who have you seen?"

"James Brown, twice. The Tempts, Gladys Knight, Joe Tex. I saw Brenda Queen and the Jacks too, the last time they were through. I'm sorry it had to happen anywhere, but here of all --"

Crowe turned to him again. This time he kept his eyes fixed on Katz's.

"I'm sorry it happened here too," he said. "But that's about all I'm sorry about. That miserable bitch had it coming to her."

The look on Katz's face made him laugh.

"Get hip, sonny. There's all kinds of people would've been happy to pull that trigger. Ain't no secret about that."

"Who would want to kill her? Why?"

"You say you're a detective?"

"I didn't. I'm not. I'm a patrolman, just, like I said, wanting to help out."

"Here it is. Help him out. I'm done with y'all."

Crowe handed him a card. Tom Wallace, Detective, 9th precinct, with a phone number.

"Thanks, I'll give him a call. As long as I'm here, though, can you show me what happened?"

Crowe folded his arms, sighed, and rested his butt on the desk. After a long moment contemplating something, he cocked his head at Katz.

"Those shows you saw? You pay full price?"

"Sure," Katz said. Crowe just stared at him.

"Just about every time, really."

Still with the stare.

"Okay, once. Maybe."

47

Crowe shook his head.

"You too honest to be a cop. Better watch yourself. Come on, I'll show you what happened."

6

Crowe led Katz halfway back up the hall to a door on the left. While he sorted through his keys, Katz took in a small framed black and white photograph hanging cockeyed on the wall across from the door. He leaned in to get a better look at the magnificent building it pictured. A statue of someone graced the top. A story below, lit posts flanked a large window just above a beautiful arch that sheltered a set of huge wooden double doors. Decorative windows ran across all three floors.

"Mr. Crowe," he asked. "What's this?"

"That's where you're standing."

"What do you mean?"

"That's the Howard Theatre, sonny."

Katz pictured the entrance he just came through, a pair of red metal doors under a tin canopy suspended by wires from a concrete wall.

"Are you serious?"

"If I'm lyin', I'm dyin'. Look close there," he said, pointing to the arch, "see what it says? 'Howard Theatre'."

Katz leaned in and saw that it did. He pointed to the statue at the top.

"And who's that?"

"That's Apollo, God of Music. Ever wonder why the Apollo up in New York's called the Apollo? Now you know." He pointed at an instrument in his hands. "And he's playing a lyre or some shit, see? Maybe it's a bass guitar, I don't know."

"When did it look like that?"

"1910, when it was built. Stayed that way up to 1941 when some fool got the idea to slick it up the way it looks today. Bad idea, I think, but what do I know? I just work here."

He found the key. He pushed Katz up a short flight of steps, then motioned him to hold there a second. He disappeared into the darkness.

Suddenly, lights bathed the stage directly in front of Katz. He shielded his eyes and made his way slowly forward to the center of the floor. He turned to face the seats. Here he was, Jake Katz, standing where James Brown, Otis Redding, Wilson Pickett, Smokey Robinson, and Brenda Queen stood. He looked down at the thousand scuff marks and chips all around him, the lasting impressions of years of spin moves, splits, and all manner of syncopated rhythm. He could barely breathe. Crowe came to his side.

"Little different view from up here, huh?"

He swept his arm across the view.

"Twelve hundred seats out there, including the balcony and the eight boxes. Can't tell you the last time we filled 'em up, though. Maybe Duke Ellington did, before my time, but no one since, not even James."

Katz took it all in, awestruck.

"I can't believe I'm here," he said.

"You want to audition? Got a little Righteous Brother in you?"

Katz was still transfixed by the scars on the floor. Was that David Ruffin's heel mark? Jackie Wilson's shoe polish? He struggled to remember he was here on business.

"So what happened? How did it start?"

"I was back in the office while Watty was doin' the intros --"

"Watty?"

"Irwin C. Watson, the comedian?"

"Oh, sure, I love him." Irwin C. Watson was an urbane, slow-talking comic who built to his punch lines with long moments of silence. Katz had seen him emcee a couple of shows here and at the Uptown in Philly.

"What's that one?" he said. "Oh, yeah, 'I used to date a girl had all these little circles all over her body. From where guys were touchin' her with ten-foot poles.'"

Crowe snorted. "Yeah, I heard that one a few times myself. Anyhow, I got the radio on, listening to the news station, WAVA, I think it is and all of a sudden they break in with the news that Dr. King had been shot, probably right around 7:30. I was so mad, so upset, I didn't know whether to cry or kick the wall down. Watty comes back and sees me and asks what's up and I tell him and he starts bawling like a baby. We hold on to each other a little bit and then I tell him he can't say anything up here about it because the people would go crazy. It was killing him not to do it but he didn't and we almost got through the whole show when some of the fool kids waiting in line for the 10 o'clock show came busting through the doors and down into the aisles here and over there" -- he pointed to the aisle they had come down and the aisle to their left -- "and they start yellin' and screamin' 'Dr. King is dead' and 'Whitey's gonna pay' and everyone gets wild and starts cryin' and screamin', jumpin' 'round. Watty and Brenda are up there, trying to calm 'em down, get quiet but it's no use. And then some smoke starts driftin' in from somewhere out on the street -- no fire here, you can see that -- but the people really go crazy then, screamin' "Fire!" and tramplin' all over each other to get out. Wonder ain't more of 'em dead."

"When did you hear the shots?"

"Right then, while everyone was screamin' and pushin'. I was back over there where we came up and I hear a shot from somewhere up there in the back" – he pointed to the top of the center aisle – "and then another two or maybe three, I really can't say, back from up on the left there, and then I hear Watty calling out 'Brenda! Brenda!' and I turn 'round and she's on her back, maybe halfway between the

51

two of us, right over there. You can see right where she bled out."

He pointed to a long, ragged crimson streak about ten feet to their right, a few feet further back from the apron. They walked over to it and looked at the last that was left of Brenda Queen. Katz didn't know if he was more overwhelmed by the moment or the flood of questions pouring through his mind.

"You don't think it was just her bad luck? Just the wrong place at the wrong time?"

"I guess I just been around too long, know too much to believe that."

"Why? What do you know?"

Crowe leaned in to read the name tag over Katz's shirt pocket.

"Officer Katz, my momma told me never to speak ill of the dead, so I'm gonna respect that and let you find all that out from somebody else."

"Like who?"

"Oh, there's plenty of somebodies be happy to rattle on to you. Won't be a problem findin' 'em. She grew up in Baltimore."

"But if I have to start somewhere, where should I start?"

Crowe considered the question a moment, then headed back to the steps. When he got there, he turned back to Katz.

"You might chat with one or two of the Jacks. I bet Edward'd have a few things to tell you, maybe ask him to tell you 'bout Jerome and her. See where that takes you."

7

Katz slogged up the steps to the second floor, leaned into the door at the landing, and listed towards the door of his apartment straight ahead. He was still fumbling with the keys when Lisa pulled the door open and threw herself around him.

"Oh thank God! You're back! I've been up all night waiting for you!"

He held her tight and they swayed slowly together for a good long moment. He gave her a long kiss filled with love, passion, and relief. He was happy to have the night behind him, happier still to be home, with her.

She gently pushed him through the door and over to the couch. She sat him down, then knelt in front of him. The only color in his eyes was red.

"You look so tired! You want some coffee?"

"No, thanks, I'm going to need some sleep soon."

"Are you okay? What was it like out there? I was so worried!"

He started to tell her but could feel himself drifting away. Before he got to the part about the cavalry coming down 14th St., he was out cold.

She got a blanket from the bedroom and laid it over him. She liked the innocence that filled his face again when he slept, his troubles – their troubles – sliding away. It was the face she fell in love with their junior year at GW. Thinking of the first time she saw it brought the same smile to her face every time.

She remembered exactly what she was wearing: a blazing yellow Villager cable knit with a paisley kerchief tied around her neck, roomy forest green bellbottoms, and desert boots. Not what she would have picked if she knew she'd be meeting her future husband that afternoon, but perfect for walking to Georgetown with her friend Sharon. A pay phone started to ring in a parking lot just past 24th and Pennsylvania.

"That's weird," Sharon said, but went over to pick it up anyhow. She said hello, then got the strangest expression on her face, somewhere between confusion and total shock. She held out the phone to Lisa and said "It's for you."

Lisa freaked out.

"What! How's it for me?"

"The guy asked for you. He said 'Hi, can I talk to Lisa please?' I'm serious!"

I'm in the Twilight Zone, she remembered thinking, but she took the phone anyhow.

"Hello?" she said.

"Hi, Lisa. You don't know me but I'm in your poli sci class and I just wanted to say hi."

She didn't know what to say but before she could figure anything out, the guy on the other end said "That sweater looks very nice on you, really goes with your pants."

She put her hand over the receiver and told Sharon what he said.

"Are you kidding me? How does he know that?"

They looked both ways down the sidewalk, then across the street to the apartment building at 2424. On the fourth floor, they saw a group of guys waving at them. Jake was the guy holding the phone. A few days later, he introduced himself again in class and things took off from there.

She was a psych major but he always kidded her about coming to GW to get her MRS degree. That might have been true but she never let him know it. When they met, they were both virgins and if she had left it up to him, they might still be. As funny and glib as he was, he had no feel for romance, so she had to lead the way. Fortunately for both of them, he was a willing student and sex was never a problem for them, before or after they married right after graduation in '67.

But there were other problems. To her, the biggest problem was that Jake wasn't sticking with what he called the game plan. The game plan was for him to get a job then start law school next September. GW was holding a spot for him and she had worked it all out. If they could squirrel away two paychecks and keep their social life on hold for a year, they'd have enough money to pay for law school and still eat. That meant that some things, like a baby, would have to wait.

To Jake, though, the problem was that Lisa didn't really understand what she called his "fascination" with police work. She knew it had some connection to what happened to his dad but she never appreciated just how much it motivated him day in and day out, mostly, he had to concede, because he never told her.

His father was murdered ten years and nine days ago. He remembered the last time he heard his voice, like it was this morning. "Tatelah" he called him and asked for this mother. Then gone, forever.

When he didn't come home that night, his mother called the Middletown Township police and told them all she knew. He was collecting debts in Trenton. He called her at 6:30 and said he'd be home by 8. Now it was 10 and she hadn't heard from him. He always called when he'd be late so she shouldn't worry. Now she was beyond worry, she was sure something terrible had happened. When they asked for information about the car he was driving, she dug out the papers and recited it to them in a trembling voice.

They told her they would call the Trenton police and ask them to be on the lookout for the car. The next day, a Trenton policeman, Sgt. Wolczyk, called to tell her they found the car, in an alley off Hudson St., and that a Township police officer would pick her up so she could look it over and tell them if she saw anything unusual. The whole way over, Katz sat next to her, trying to squeeze a little life into her cold hand but she didn't say a word, just rocked and sobbed like she'd done since the minute she made the call to the police that was the beginning of the end of the life she loved.

The sobs broke into a bawl when they pulled up behind the Ford. A beefy policeman with a florid complexion opened her door and stood beside it, his hands clasped below his belt, waiting for whenever she felt ready to get out. Katz got out his side and came around the back of the squad car.

"Sergeant Wolczyk," the cop said and extended his hand.

"Jake Katz," Jake said and shook it. Then he turned to stand next to him, hands clasped below his belt too and waited for his mother to pull herself together. When she finally nodded at Katz, he reached in and helped her out. Sgt. Wolczyk stepped back to let them by.

Fanny stood behind the Ford, stricken, slowly shaking her head. Katz and the Sergeant each held her by an elbow until Katz saw the stain on the ground just past the front of the car. He nodded to Sgt. Wolczyk, who nodded back and tightened his grip. Katz let her go and walked up to the spot. He looked down at an almost perfect circle maybe three feet across of something dark red going on brown with splatters of the same shade flecked around it.

Corporal Barrows, the Township policeman who drove them over, walked to his side.

"Is that blood?," Katz asked.

"Looks like it but I really don't know."

"Who would know?"

"The Sergeant can tell you exactly what they do over here but it's probably just what we do. They scrape some specimens and send it to a lab, and they tell you what it is."

"Can they tell if it was my father's?"

Corporal Barrows shook his head no.

"They can tell you if it's human or animal, give you a blood type, but that's about it."

About a week later, Sgt. Wolczyk called to bring them up to date on the investigation. Fanny picked up the phone in the living room. Katz picked up the one in her bedroom.

"Okay, so first of all," the Sergeant said, "the blood on the ground? It is human and it's O positive." Katz heard his mother gasp.

"That was Sam's type!," she said. "Oh *Gottenyu!*"

"That doesn't necessarily mean it's his, Mrs. Katz. Lots of people are O positive."

"Don't!" she hissed at him. "Just don't! That's his blood! You know that's his blood!" She dissolved into a wail of grief.

"Mrs. Katz," the Sergeant tried to break in, "Mrs. Katz, we really can't be sure."

"You can't but I can!" she bit back.

"Mom," Katz said, "I think he means that they can't use it in court." He heard them say that on Dragnet all the time, but he wasn't really sure it was true or even what it meant.

"Your son's right, Mrs. Katz. It's not something we can use as evidence is all I meant."

Katz heard a phone slam down, then watched his mother storm into the bedroom and root around in her purse until she came up with a handkerchief.

"Get off that phone with that liar!," she screamed at him. "He knows that's your father's blood but he's not telling us! But I know, I know! Hang up, Jake, now!"

But Jake needed to know everything anyone knew about how his father died, whether they could prove it or not, whether his mother wanted him to know or not.

He shook his head at his mother for the first time in his life.

"What else?," he asked Sergeant Wolczyk.

His mother punched her chest with the hand holding the handkerchief and started to say something but her mouth just hung there, open, her eyes filled with shock. Then she spun and left the room, leaving Katz too overwhelmed by his own *chutzpah* to hear what the Sergeant was saying.

"I'm sorry," he said. "Can you say that again?"

"Sure. Your father had a pizza that night, at De Lorenzo's on Hudson, about three, four blocks from where we found the car, sometime between six-thirty and seven. Then he talked to a guy who owed Dunham's some money, over on Emory, about two blocks from the restaurant."

"Is that the guy who killed him?"

"Again, Jake – can I call you Jake?"

"Sure."

"We don't know anything for sure just yet, but it doesn't look like it. The guy said they talked out on the corner for five minutes tops, then your father headed off towards where we found the car."

"But he could be lying, right?"

"He could, but his wife told us the same story about when your father showed up and how long her husband -- Gino -- was gone."

"But she'd lie to protect him, wouldn't she?"

"Yeah, she would. But we also got a few neighbor ladies who saw him walk up the block with your father then walk back down alone a few minutes later."

Katz wasn't so ready to let this Gino off the hook.

"But he had a reason to kill my dad." He paused a second to swallow hard, hearing those words come out of his mouth. "Maybe he didn't want to pay him and beat him up or something."

"I hear what you're saying, Jake, and that's good thinking but here's what we know. He was in the Navy, got an honorable discharge. He's got no record, committed no crimes except once when he was in junior high, he got caught stealing a soft pretzel from a bowling alley. He works a broiler at Jerry's over the bridge in Morrisville. We really don't think he had anything to do with your dad disappearing."

Katz didn't like hearing that his dad disappeared. It reminded him of some of the phone calls his mother had in the last few days. She was talking in Yiddish but he had heard enough of it over the years that he could piece together what was going on. Some people were saying that his dad wasn't really dead, that he just took off, with everything in their bank account.

"Disappear? Is that what you think happened? My father just disappeared?"

"You're asking me, no, that's not what I think. But I don't know he didn't and I'm a cop so I can't count anything out, or in, until I get all the facts in front of me. And I got to tell you, Jake, people disappear in Trenton and everywhere else all the time. Just around the time your dad -- didn't show up, a guy who worked at a brewery here just never showed up again either, at his house, at work, nowhere. It happens, believe me."

"And do you ever find out what happened?"

"Honestly, Jake, the dagos and the coloreds? They usually take care of their own problems and we never find out anything. Your people, though, they want us to know, to keep digging, and we will. We'll stick with it, kid, I promise you that."

But they never did find out. Was he killed by that deadbeat? Robbed on the street? Kidnapped and left somewhere to die? Once he got his license, Katz drove to that alley every weekend to look at all that was left of his father and wait for some bolt of inspiration to strike him, show him how all the puzzle pieces fit together, but it never happened. The spot shrunk and lost color to the point where it was invisible if you didn't know it was there and then the summer of his senior year in high school they re-paved the alley and he never went back.

The questions ate at him every day. He watched every TV cop show, lawyer show, listening, looking for clues that might help him solve his own mystery. Joe Friday always got his guy in a half hour, Perry Mason took an hour but they always found their man and explained why. He longed for someone who would do that for him. He longed to do it himself. He longed to be as much of his father as he could. Even though he never grew into his size, he had his old man's attitude. He wasn't insulted, but proud when he overheard his high school football coach tell another coach to find playing time for that "scrappy little Hebe."

Jake knew why Lisa thought he wanted a baby and wanted one now.

"Your mother," she kept telling him, "Your mother wants one, to give her something new to love to replace what she lost." More than once, when things got heated she even called him a momma's boy but Katz denied it every time, mostly because he could never tell her the real reason:

He wanted to stay on the force.

Why was complicated. Redemption for his father was one reason, and one that he could maybe make Lisa understand. But she'd never understand the other reasons, especially that he wasn't sure he even wanted to go to law school. He only applied because it would buy him another three years to figure out what to do with his life -- if he was lucky enough to get in. Once he did, he had to go. He'd be crazy not to. He knew that – except for the other thing he couldn't tell her.

He loved being a cop. He didn't plan on it. The job was just something to make some money and buy some time. But it hit him sometime early on, maybe when he stepped in and saved that little queer a beating at Dupont Circle, or maybe the first time he testified and saw the mugger he arrested go to jail, or maybe when he let Mattie with the face smashed in by her boyfriend stay with them until he found a cousin to take her in. Even now, with the city exploding all around him, he still loved it. Maybe it was because it was so easy to get a paycheck just for being what he was raised to be: a *mensch*.

But telling Lisa all that was something he couldn't bring himself to do. He didn't want to hurt her, didn't want to ruin what they had. So the baby became his way out. Then he'd have to stay on the force to keep earning money to support his new family.

Lisa watched him sleep. She knew something was up but she couldn't find a way to make him tell her. It was eating at her more and more. Now she watched herself throw off his blanket, shake him by the shoulders, and scream at him "Tell them you're coming!" over and over again.

Then she woke with a start.

He was still sleeping so peacefully. She envied him, loved him, and hated him all at once.

8

Lisa was shaking him by his shoulders and telling him something, he knew that much.

"Jake, Jake, sweetie, Floyd's on the phone. You have to go back in."

"What?" he mumbled. "Why?"

She stretched the phone cord as far as it could go and wedged the receiver under his ear.

"Ikey, we gotta go. They're all over the city. I'll meet you at the station."

Katz sat up and the phone fell to the floor. He could hear Floyd yelling something from down there. He leaned over and yelled "Yeah, yeah, I'm going," then fell back in the chair.

Lisa hung the phone up and knelt next to him. She slowly rubbed his bristly hair.

"What time is it?" he asked.

"A little after noon." He had barely slept two hours.

"What's going on out there? Do you know?"

"Maury Povich just said Stokely Carmichael gave a speech up at Howard and the crowd was coming down 7th Street starting to cause trouble."

He sat up and rubbed his eyes, then stood up to see what he was wearing. He was still in uniform. Lisa stood up and hugged him tight.

"I am so scared," she said.

So am I, he thought, but he said "It'll be okay. I'll take care of myself, I promise."

He kissed her on the forehead and headed for the bedroom. Two minutes later, he kissed her again and headed out the door.

A two-story red brick building that looked more like a house than a police station, 1st Precinct headquarters stood at the corner of 6th and New York Northwesst. Katz had to wait for a string of patrol cars to roar past him up 6th before he could turn into the parking lot. When he pulled in, Floyd was there waiting for him. He rolled down the window.

"What's going on?"

"Looks like last night was just a warmup. They're torchin' everything today. Come on."

They took their own cruiser this time, Floyd at the wheel, shooting up through Chinatown. Tall plumes of black smoke curled over them heading east. Sirens drowned out any other noise. They made a left on K and followed the line of cars ahead across 7th. A Lieutenant motioned them to pull onto the sidewalk in front of the library. They hopped out and caught the riot gear thrown their way off the back of a bus. They hustled across Mount Vernon Square to the corner of 7th and Mass, downtown to their backs, the fires and God knows what else to their front. Katz didn't have to be told the mission: Keep them from coming downtown.

They moved up 7th in loose ranks maybe fifteen men across. For a few blocks, things looked good. The streets were clear. He could even hear Jarvie on his bullhorn, standing on the hood of a cruiser blocking M, urging them to stay cool, stay cool, keep the peace, hold your fire if you're not in danger. He couldn't hear the muttering this time but he knew what they all were thinking. He was thinking it too.

Unlike his last walk on 7th, he took the time to look at each of the storefronts they passed. Macklin's, Leventhal's, Becker's, so many Jewish names. He knew that 7th St. had been the heart of the Jewish neighborhood in D.C., before the Negroes moved in and the Jews moved out. They kept their businesses there though, selling food, liquor, clothes, and appliances to the new residents. Many of the merchants saw it as a *mitzvah* – a good thing – to serve the underprivileged and were willing to suffer crime and high insurance rates to stay. But most of their customers thought the Jews were gouging them and keeping Negro-owned businesses from taking hold. Katz passed a furniture store with a sign in the window reading "We Cheat You Right!" Any other day, it would've made him laugh. Today, he just hoped the owner wasn't a Jew.

A huge group of Negroes, mostly high school age, swarmed down the street towards them just before R. The ranks in front of Katz ran to meet them, sticks swinging. The smoke was thicker and closer and he could smell whatever was in flames up ahead. Behind him, he heard windows smash. He spun and looked towards Leventhal's just in time to see a mattress sail out of the second floor onto the street. Kids streamed in the front doors empty handed and streamed out with their arms full of blankets, pillows, chairs, tables, and anything else they could carry. Katz and the cops around him just watched. Maybe they were all like him, too stunned by the bastards' brass balls, too overwhelmed by the sheer number of them to even move.

Floyd had a different take. He looked at Katz and shrugged.

"If we can't shoot 'em, fuck it. Let 'em run buck wild."

A full liquor bottle hitting him square between the shoulders changed his mind. He had no idea who threw it but could care less. He ran into the mob surging through the gaping entrance to Leventhal's and crowned anyone in his path. Katz and a horde of cops followed him in and managed to clear the entrance. Katz chased a guy in a purple sportcoat and a do-rag down 7th but he couldn't catch him. When he turned to look back up 7th, the enormity of what they were up against hit him full blast. A fog of smoke and fire blotted out the horizon. Hundreds, maybe thousands of Negroes swarmed in and out of stores on every block. The cops

64

looked like tiny blue islands in an ocean of chaos. There was no way they could stop what was roaring all around them.

Mayor Washington had figured that out too, but it took another two hours before the troop carriers came roaring up 7th and 14th and H St. Northeast, deploying dozens of National Guardsmen on practically every corner. Katz was too exhausted to raise his arm but he mentally saluted all the guys jumping out the back of the deuce-and-a-half that slammed to a stop just behind him at N. He could see a line of the hoop-backed trucks all the way down 7th St., stretching back into the smoke engulfing downtown. He felt it hit him right then that life would never be the same for any of them, black or white, from now on. Too many lines had been crossed, too much had been shattered, broken forever.

9

Katz spent the rest of Friday on his feet. When he wasn't patrolling 7th and the alleys branching off every block, he was guarding the fire trucks or helping firemen pull hose. The strangest moment was when someone who said he owned Becker's asked him to throw a tear gas grenade into the store to "keep the colored bastards out" till he had a chance to clean it up. He declined. Mercifully, the looting stopped as soon as the Guard showed up so he didn't have to run anymore but the ache radiating down his legs and the pain in his knee kept him silently begging to just go home and lay down. Law school was looking better every minute.

The smoke finally started to lift, giving him the weird sensation of night turning to day as the afternoon dragged on. He finally saw sunlight break through low in the sky, silhouetting the Monument still standing no more than twenty blocks away. He felt tears well in his eyes. That was what drew him to Washington in the first place, the splendor, the grandeur, the feeling that he would be at the heart of a fight for truth and justice, answering the challenge that President Kennedy had thrown down when he called on every American to ask what they could do for their country. He never dreamed that saving Washington itself was what he'd do.

As the sun disappeared, they got relief but just until midnight. Then they'd redeploy to back up the Guard. He and Floyd dragged their way back down 7th to K. They took their time driving back to the station.

Katz fell into the swivel chair behind the desk he shared with junior officers on the other shifts. It rolled back across the tiled floor until he dug his heels in and duck-walked it back under the desk. He let his head fall back and waited for the sleep he knew would come to overtake him.

Jackie, the front desk clerk with the Supremes hairdo, tapped him on the forehead.

"Hello? You awake?"

"I am now."

"You got a phone call a couple hours ago. Said he was calling you back."

She waved a pink message note in front of his eyes. He took it and saw Detective Wallace had called him. It took him a few seconds to remember that he was the detective investigating the Brenda Queen shooting at the Howard. He got up and looked for an empty office with a phone, then dialed the number.

"Wallace."

Katz thought he sounded like a Negro, which he hadn't expected.

"Hi, this is Jake Katz. Thanks for call --"

"The fuck you doin' at the Howard?"

"Excuse me?"

"Why you talkin' to anyone up there?"

"I talked to Mr. Crowe. He told me to call you--"

"OK, so now you called me. Now butt the fuck out."

"I wasn't butting in. I --"

"You buckin' for detective? You want my job? That what's goin' on? Not enough of you motherfuckers got it already?"

"Detective, hold on, hold on. I loved Brenda Queen's music. I'd seen her at the Howard. I just wanted to help somehow, whatever you think I could –"

"You wanna help? Do your own fuckin' job and leave me do mine."

Katz thought he'd see if Wallace was doing his own fuckin' job.

"Did Mr. Crowe tell you he thinks she was murdered? Did he tell you to talk to the Jacks?"

67

"Who you think you are, man? I don't answer to you. Stay outta my case, you got it?"

The receiver slammed down before Katz could tell him he got it.

And he wasn't staying out of it.

10

Sunday night, the only signs of life on 7th Street were the Guardsmen lining the sidewalks all the way up. The stores or what were left of them were all dark and even the smoke had disappeared. Katz turned right on T and parked in front of Cecilia's at the corner of Wiltberger Street, just past the Howard. That's where Edward Jackson said he'd meet him at 7:30.

Katz thought a long time about whether to take the cruiser and go in uniform or drive his own car and wear civvies. The deciding factor was the unknown. He had never been to Cecilia's and didn't want to find out the hard way who its patrons were and what they might think of a white cop showing up a day after the riots. Edward knew why he was there so he tucked his badge into his wallet, put on a denim CPO jacket and jeans, and gave the Merc a rare run uptown.

Whatever went on in Cecilia's would stay a secret till he went through the door. Glass brick windows kept the inside in and the outside out. He looked both ways up and down T. As deserted as 7th. He pulled the heavy metal door and stepped inside.

The longest bar he ever saw grabbed his eye first, running the length of the room down the Wiltberger Street side under a bank of mirrors. A jukebox down the wall across from it played the Marvelettes' "Hunter Gets Captured By The Game".

Two women in white blouses and black skirts perched on the bar stools closest to him, chatting with a pretty, soft-featured woman with short brown hair, maybe in her mid-forties, behind the bar. When she spoke to him, the others turned to take him in. They were knockouts. The taller one scanned him up and down, the other just stared into his eyes, as if they'd tell her why he was really there before he lied about it.

"Here for something to drink, or something to eat?" the woman behind the bar asked.

"I'm not sure yet," he said. "I'm meeting Edward Jackson here. He's one of the Jacks, with Brenda Queen?"

"I know who Edward is," she said. "I suspect he'll be here in a minute. Take a seat anywhere you like."

He thanked her and headed for one of the tables past the bar. He took the one furthest from the door, in front of a stairway and sat facing the door so he could keep an eye out for Edward. An older couple at the table to his right both glanced his way then resumed their conversation. The rest of the tables were empty.

The short woman at the bar came his way, fingers tapping a light steady beat on every stool she passed. He followed her fingers, then her rolling hips and the breasts swelling into her blouse before he slowly made his way up to her face, a sharp chin and high cheekbones under dark coffee eyes and smooth processed hair pulled back tight and firm. As she stood above him, her look asked him if he enjoyed the show.

She handed him the menu, then pulled the other chair out and took a seat across from him. She leaned in and whispered, "You a cop?"

His eyes darted to the couple at the next table. They kept on talking.

"It's that obvious?" he asked. She shrugged.

"I figure a white man I never saw before wanting to talk to Edward a couple days after Brenda got shot just might be, you know?"

"Very sharp. You might make a good cop yourself."

"Oh, yeah, that'll be the day," she laughed. "I'm Yvonne. What can I call you, besides 'Officer'?"

70

"Jake Katz." He offered his hand and she laid hers in it.

"Pleased," she said.

"You know Edward so you must've known Brenda too, I bet."

"Oh, sure. I didn't really know her but I saw enough, heard enough, to know enough."

"What do you know?"

"That she had a rough time on this earth. Even with all the singin' and all the glory, she was a tortured soul. Couldn't help but see that."

"How? What do you mean?"

"I guess I mean that none of us out here know how tough it is to be in that business, especially for a lady. Everybody wants to get close to you, get a piece of you, offer you every temptation under the sun. Everybody say, 'Oh, that Brenda, she a tough cookie, she mean and nasty'. Well, maybe that was the only way she could protect herself, take care of what was hers. You see what I mean?"

Katz nodded, trying to square his image of the ethereal, silky Brenda Queen with the miserable bitch and tortured soul that Em and Yvonne said she was.

"You want something to drink while you wait?," she asked.

"Just a Coke, please. Thanks, Yvonne."

She got up and he enjoyed watching her circle behind the bar.

"Happy Birthday, Chuck!" was written on the mirror down his end in large loopy gold and red letters. He looked out at the room. Didn't look like anyone was celebrating anything tonight.

He took a longer look at the couple at the next table and two men taking stools at the bar to see if maybe anyone else who was on the bill might be there. No one looked

71

familiar and no wonder. There was no chance the Howard would be open any time soon and probably not for a long time either. If the slim crowd here tonight was any indication, Cecilia's was heading the same way.

He saw the lady behind the bar nod to somebody behind him. He turned to see Edward Jackson.

Katz recognized him right away. He was one of the two rail-thin Jacks who always flanked the huskier one. Even off stage, he was elegant, his slick hair parted crisply on the right, a line of a mustache groomed perfectly. He wore a black sport jacket over a black and white pinstripe shirt and flared gray pants.

"Officer Katz, I presume," he said. Katz rose to shake his hand and gestured him to the empty seat.

"I was keeping an eye out for you," Katz said, pointing to the door. "How'd I miss you?"

"Because I came down the stairs," he said, pointing back over Katz' shoulder. "I stay in one of the rooms up there."

"Did Brenda stay here too?" Katz asked.

"No, the rest of them always stayed at the Whitelaw, over on 13th Street. Nice place, but I like to stay here. Go across the street, do the gig, come on back, and rest up for the next one. No muss, no fuss."

"Plus, everybody here pampers him all day long, but he won't tell you that."

Katz looked up to see the woman behind the bar now behind Edward, squeezing his shoulders.

Edward reached back to pat her hands.

"Aw, now, Cecilia," he said. "I was just gettin' to that part."

Katz stood up and reached across the table to shake her hand. She reached out and squeezed his hand gently.

"Cecilia Scott," she said.

"This is Officer Katz," Edward said. "He's here to talk with me about Brenda."

"You know Lieutenant Pittman?" she asked Katz.

"No, I don't," he said.

"Patrolman Scott? White man? He's here all the time."

"No, I'm still kind of new. I just started last summer."

"Picked a heck of a time to be a cop around here, didn't you?," she said, shaking her head. "Terrible what happened to Brenda. She was in here just the night before she was killed."

"Just like Sam," Edward said.

Brenda came around between them.

"You know, I thought the same thing myself," she said. "You keep that to yourself, if you please. We don't need one more reason for people to stay away."

"Sam?," Katz said.

Edward pulled a zipper across his mouth. Cecilia rolled her eyes at him, then pulled a chair from the table behind him and took a seat between them. She turned to Katz.

"Sam Cooke. He was here the night before he died too."

Katz was stunned. He knew Sam Cooke had been killed a few years ago, supposedly by a prostitute, but he didn't know where.

"Really?," he said. "He got killed in D.C.?"

"No," Cecilia said, "in Los Angeles. But he was here the night before he went out there. Left at midnight, gave me a kiss on the cheek, says he's heading to LA, see me the next time. Two days later, I hear on the radio, he's dead."

She stared at the table and shook her head.

"And now this. And the riots. I've been here fifteen years. I got Tina and Isabel depending on me. I am so worried."

"Are they your daughters?" Katz asked.

"Tina's the daughter. Isabel's my sister. She lives with us upstairs. Good God Almighty, what do you have in store for us?"

She rubbed her hands together anxiously until Edward reached over to wrap his around them.

"It'll be okay, Cecilia. It'll be okay."

They sat quietly while he stroked her hands. After a minute, Edward winked at Katz and moved his chair closer to Cecilia's. He put his arm around her shoulders and whispered in her ear loud enough for Katz to hear too.

"Maybe, just maybe, this is the time you ought to stop playin' so hard to get with James, huh?"

She stared at him, not understanding at first. Then she got hot. She threw his arm off and reached out to slap him. He ducked away and cowered behind his arms, laughing at his excellent joke.

"Oh!," she cried. "You are a horrible man!"

"Cecilia!," Katz heard behind him. He turned to see Yvonne pointing up the steps.

"Tina's calling for you," she said.

"Tell her I'll be right up," Cecilia said. She turned back to Edward and leveled a finger at his face.

"And you tell that young man you are just joking. You do it now!"

"I will, I will," he laughed. "Go tend to your daughter."

They watched her storm up the stairs. When they heard the thunder subside, Katz turned back to Edward.

"James?," he said. "James Brown?"

"The one and only," Edward said. "He's got a real crush on her. It's a blast watching them together. Better show than on stage sometimes."

"Wow!," Katz said. He was dying to hear more but made himself reach into his back pocket and pull out his wallet. He flipped it open to show Edward his badge.

"Maybe I ought to get back to business," he said. "Thanks for giving me the time, Mr. Jackson."

Edward threw him a mock salute and reached into his jacket pocket. He pulled out a pack of Salems, slid one out, lit it, and tossed the pack onto the table.

"Call me Edward. Always happy to help our men in blue. Just one minute."

He looked back to the bar and held up a finger. The tall bar maid nodded. Edward turned back to Katz.

"So," he said, "what can I do for you?"

"First, let me say how sorry I am that Brenda, Miss Queen, was killed. I was a big fan."

"Appreciate that. It's a hard loss."

He took a long draw from the cigarette and tapped it on the lip of the ash tray.

"You know she was family too."

"No, I didn't."

"Cousin of mine, and James – Jackson, not Brown." Katz pictured the group and, for the first time, saw the resemblance between Brenda Queen and her two thin Jacks.

"And Jerome?" He was the heavy set one with the ringlets piled high on top.

Edward shook his head.

"Naw, he's just an old family friend. Jerome Terry. The four of us grew up on the same block in Baltimore, Eutaw Place, right off North Avenue?"

"That's amazing."

"One word for it."

The bar maid laid a glass with two inches of something brown in it in front of Edward. He thanked her and raised his glass to Katz. Katz clinked it with his Coke bottle.

"Edward," he said, "I want to ask you a few questions but I need to tell you that I'm not the guy officially investigating what happened, so you may have to talk to a detective too."

Edward took a long pull on his Salem, inhaled it all, and squinted at Katz through the smoke curling off the tip.

"So why am I talking to you?"

" I know it sounds stupid but I love your music and loved seeing you at the Howard, so I just feel like I have to try and help find who killed her however I can."

Jackson took that in, then shrugged.

"So what do you want to know?"

"When I talked to Mr. Crowe, he seemed to think it wasn't just a random shot that killed Miss Queen, but maybe somebody who wanted to kill her taking advantage of the situation."

Edward's face didn't give away what he was thinking. He took a sip of his drink and put it back down, looking at Katz the whole time, saying nothing. Katz pressed the point.

"He thought you might tell me who wanted her dead."

"Is that right? And did Mr. Crowe tell you who that might be?"

"He said you might have something to say about her and Jerome."

Edward swirled the ice around in his glass and looked down the bar. The bar maids were chatting again at the far end. The men on the stools were engrossed in their own conversation about what their kids got into the night before. The couple at the next table was gone.

He turned back to Katz.

"If Jerome was kin, you wouldn't be hearin' any of this."

Katz nodded and waited.

"The two of them had a thing for each other, pretty much startin' back in high school. Carried on and off right up till now, or at least till, you know."

"Were they fighting? Did something happen between them?"

Edward laughed.

"No, nothin', unless you count Walker."

"Who's Mr. Walker?"

"Not Mr. Walker, Mr. Thomas. Walker's his first name."

"So how did Mr. Thomas get involved?"

"He was our manager."

"Okay."

"And Brenda's husband."

Edward watched Katz take this in.

"Oh. So, what, he found out about them?"

"He had to know, but really, if Jerome's face was on a dollar bill, he woulda cared a whole lot more."

Katz looked confused so Edward spelled it out for him.

"She was more Walker's meal ticket than anything else. I don't know when she stopped being his lady but it was a long time ago, I can tell you that much."

"Was he there the night she was shot?"

"Oh, yeah. He never missed a show, always wanted to see the gate count, make sure no one was rippin' him off. He always thought everyone was robbin' him blind -- like it was his money, not ours, probably because he figured they the same as him -- the record company, the promoter, the house, Mr. Reynolds."

"Who's Mr. Reynolds?"

"Albert Reynolds, the accountant, friend of the family since forever. Still up there in Baltimore. He's a Morehouse man, really knows how to invest the money. Watched every dime, watched Walker too, even more. Not a finer man among us."

Katz tried to tally up what he knew. Brenda Queen was married to Walker Thomas but having a thing with Jerome. Thomas could care less about that but a lot more about the money. Reynolds was watching him watch the money.

"It seems Mr. Thomas might have a lot to do with this."

"Depends what you mean by 'this'. If you're talkin' 'bout where the money went, he's got everything to do with it. If you talkin' about who killed Brenda, that's a whole 'nother thing."

"Does he still live in Baltimore?"

"No, down here. Gold Coast. Off 16th St.?"

"Do you know if he's in town?"

"I haven't seen him in a couple of days. But I haven't been lookin' for him either."

"How about Mr. Reynolds? Do you have an address for him?"

"I don't. Walker handled all that but I don't expect you want to ask him for it. Got to be in the phone book though."

"I'll check. Anything else you think I should know?"

Edward stubbed out his cigarette and took a last sip of his drink.

"Just know what you're gettin' yourself into, that's all."

11

Back at the station house, Katz wrote up the notes of his interview with Edward. The easiest thing to do would be to just keep them to himself. A harder thing would be to pull the green copy and send it to Wallace. The hardest thing would be to pick up the phone and tell him what Edward had told him. He decided the satisfaction of letting him know he was still on the case made the hardest thing the easiest. He was actually disappointed when the clerk told him she thought he was out. He waited while she checked the sign-out sheet.

"Yep," she said, "he's at the morgue. 'Brenda Queen autopsy' it says. Can I take a message for him?"

Katz was already out of his seat and running for the cruiser.

"The morgue!" he yelled to Jackie. "Where's the morgue?"

"DC General!"

"Where's that?"

"Mass Av! Southeast!"

She watched him fly out the door.

"No sense in hurryin'," she said. "Whoever it is ain't goin' nowhere anyhow."

He threw on the siren and flashers and made it in less than ten minutes. He ran to the attendant's station.

"Brenda Queen's autopsy? Do you know where it is?"

She pointed down the hall to her left.

"Take the steps down one level and go straight back."

He sprinted down the lime green hall and nearly tripped racing down the stairs. Through the round window on the door ahead of him, he saw a heavyset black man in a dark blue suit talking to a white woman in green scrubs. He caught his breath before heading in. The room was cold.

They both turned to him at once.

"May I help you?" the woman said.

"I'm Patrolman Katz with MPD. I'm here for the Brenda Queen autopsy?"

"Then you're just in time. Do you know Detective Wallace?"

He turned to Wallace. He was a handsome heavy-set man with a modest Afro and sideburns running halfway down his cheek. His brown eyes were cold.

"We've talked on the phone," Katz said. "I think I have some more information for you."

Wallace turned back to the woman.

"Will you excuse us a second?"

"Of course."

Wallace clamped his hand on Katz's elbow and walked him back towards the door.

"You can leave now, Dick Tracy. No reason for you to be here."

"No? What if she was murdered?"

"That's why I'm here, junior. Don't need your help."

Katz pressed him. "Mr. Crowe gave me some good leads on who might have wanted her dead."

Wallace pointed a thick finger in his face. "Let me give you rule one about how a detective works, okay? A detective lets the evidence come to him. He doesn't come in with theories, especially half-assed theories, and try to make the facts fit what he thinks. That," he said, jabbing the finger into Katz's chest, "is how a dumb-ass, know-nothin', peckerwood rookie street cop thinks."

Katz pushed his hand away. "So you won't even talk to the Jacks or their accountant or anyone else who might really know what was going on with her?"

"I might, once I know there's a crime here. I'm going to have to see some real evidence before I start hearin' people jack their jaws about who might've done somethin' that never really happened."

At the sound of doors smacking open at the other side of the room, they both turned to see a male nurse wheel a gurney to a stop in the center of the room. An older man followed him through and threw a switch that made the fluorescent tubes above them shine bright white. The young man left. The nurse called over to them.

"Detective, Patrolman, this is Dr. Luke. He's the medical examiner. He'll be performing the autopsy on Miss Queen."

Katz yanked his arm from Wallace's grasp and joined them. Wallace came to his side and leaned into him. Katz leaned back and held his ground.

The nurse circled to the other side of the gurney and pulled back the lime green sheet covering Brenda Queen. Katz sucked in a breath and held it as he took in her naked body. He was distraught to see her dead, stunned to see her naked, embarrassed to be there at all. He tried to get more air but couldn't. Wallace slid him a look and shook his head. Katz fought to keep his emotions at bay. He made himself survey every inch of the body, forcing himself to dwell on the details.

The shiny bouffant he'd seen at the Howard was just a wig. Her hair was natural, cut close to the scalp. Her closed eyelids veiled the green eyes she was so famous for flashing. Maybe, he hoped, there had been some mistake, maybe this wasn't Brenda Queen after all. But there was no mistaking the high and heavy cheekbones and full lips. This was the Queen of Soul.

Dr. Luke rotated her left arm and bent closer to examine the area between the palm of her hand and the inside of the elbow. He turned to dictate something to the nurse

81

then nodded at Wallace and Katz to come closer. He pointed at the puncture marks dotting her skin all the way up.

"Hypodermic marks, some scabbed over. Been going on for a long time."

"Brenda Queen was a junkie?" Katz heard himself ask.

"Looks like it," Dr. Luke said. "We'll have to wait for the blood work to confirm."

Katz wanted to go. Now. Why had he ever come? Wallace was right. It was none of his business. He had no reason to see what he'd seen, to know what he wished he'd never known. He watched Dr. Luke examine her, feeling his way down her body, pausing to measure, to murmur something to the nurse, to proceed as a matter of course, oblivious to whoever she might have been in life. How could he do this, body after body, day after day, year after year?

Luke leaned over her chest, then moved past Wallace and Katz to the other side of the gurney where he leaned in closer. He waved them to join him.

Katz made himself ignore the fact that these were Brenda Queen's breasts and followed Luke's finger to what looked like a small, shiny cyst about an inch to the right of her left nipple.

"There it is," Luke said. Wallace nodded but Katz had to ask.

"What?"

"The bullet that probably killed her."

Katz leaned in closer. The shine was coming off a round metal tip poking through the skin. When he leaned back, Luke and the nurse rolled her body over to reveal her back. Luke crouched down, said something to the nurse, then stood up to let Katz and Wallace have their own look. Wallace got on one knee and Katz peered over his shoulder at the hole between her right shoulder blade and her spine.

"Entry wound," the doctor said, then made his measurements and announced them to the nurse. He pulled the body back to him and pushed and prodded his gloved finger into the exit wound until the bullet poked out far enough for him to pull it free. He held it up and rotated it. Wallace leaned in to look it over with him.

"I see no flattening," Dr. Luke said. "You?"

Wallace gave it an extra look, then shook his head. Luke turned to Katz, who gave him a quizzical look.

"Didn't deflect off anything," Luke said.

Katz nodded but his look didn't change. Luke spelled it out for him.

"If it was flat on one side, that'd mean it hit something before it hit her, which'd make it easier to call it an accidental homicide. Like this, still could be, but I can't rule out murder either."

Katz turned to Wallace.

"Murder. That's a crime, isn't it?"

12

Wallace blew out of the room as soon as the examination was over. Katz sprinted across the parking lot to catch up with him.

"Detective, hold up for a second!"

The detective didn't hold up.

Katz caught up to him and matched his stride.

"I called you this morning to tell you what one of the Jacks told me about why she might have been murdered."

This made Wallace hold up.

"You still talkin' to people?"

"Mr. Crowe told me Edward might have something to say about who might've wanted her dead. And he did."

Wallace shook his head and bumped past Katz, heading for a black Ford Fairlane.

"She was married to their manager, but having an affair with one of the Jacks. There may also be some funny business with the money. There might be a lot of people who had a reason to kill her."

Wallace threw open the driver's side door and threw his briefcase across the front seat. Then he turned to Katz.

"Listen, kid, where you come from, everyone might be living their little spot-free lives but where I come from -- where she came from -- everyone who climbed their way out got people they stepped on, cheated, hustled, that's just a fact of life. Doesn't make 'em all killers."

"But one of them could be. Shouldn't we at least try to find out?"

Wallace threw himself behind the wheel and snapped the ignition on.

"'We'? We a 'we' now, huh? I'm the detective here, sonny, remember? You a punk rookie. I'll take it from here, okay?"

Katz answered but he wasn't sure Wallace heard it as he peeled away, so he yelled it again, with emphasis.

"No way! Asshole!"

13

That Saturday night, Lisa and a couple of her old GW friends walked to Georgetown for dinner and some window shopping so Katz invited Schein over to watch James Brown do a concert on TV, live from Boston to keep the brothers there off the street. His bride was never a Schein fan, even before she knew he was dealing weed to Katz and half the campus. It may have had something to do with the first time they met.

Before Katz moved in with Lisa their senior year, he and Schein shared a one-bedroom at 2424 Pennsylvania. Back in the apartment after a run to Bassin's for burgers and onion rings, Katz was on the can when he heard Schein blast a fart so loud he thought it was his own for a second.

"One!" he heard from outside the door. By the time he got himself together and out into the living room, Schein was up to "Six!"

Katz took him in, lying on their lime green Goodwill shag carpet facing their 13" black and white Goodwill TV set, chin resting on his hand, watching "Hogan's Heroes," oblivious for all the world to his own titanic eruptions.

"What's the record?" Katz yelled from the far end of the room.

"Forty-nine!" Schein yelled back over another blast. "Seven!"

Katz picked up the count. Before he got to "Twenty!" he was laughing too hard to stay with him. Right after "Twenty-nine!," Lisa came through the door with a bag from Federal Market.

Katz greeted her with a quick wave. Schein greeted her with number thirty.

Katz buried his head in the corduroy sofa cushion to stifle his laughter, and duck the smell.

Schein greeted her again.

Katz lifted his head for a second to bellow "Thirty-one!" then crashed back into the cushion, his tears streaming down the ridges. He started to hiccup and could not stop.

Lisa dropped the bag on the counter and slapped a hand over her nose. She stifled a gag and stared at them in total disbelief.

"What are you doing?" she yelled. "Are you retards?"

Schein turned his head to look up at her.

"Yo. You must be Lisa." A motorboat went off in his pants but his face betrayed no sign. "I'm Schein."

"Thirty-two!" Katz cried, then turned to Lisa. "The record's forty-nine!"

"God, you're animals! Ugh!"

She bolted out the door. Schein cranked out a booming, lingering farewell.

Katz choked out most of "Thirty-three!" before totally losing it.

Lisa didn't talk to him for three days and never talked to Schein again. Katz never let her know she was in the presence of history, the night Schein topped the Babe and Maris with sixty-two.

Schein knocked on the door a little before eight. Katz could see he was high but that was the deal they made. When he interviewed for the job at MPD, one of the recruiters asked him if he did any drugs.

"Yeah," he said, "but I stopped years ago."

"'Years ago?'" the guy snorted. "When? When you were ten?"

"I don't do it any more is what I'm saying."

"Yeah, me neither," the recruiter said. "Just don't show up stoned, okay?"

87

The night he got hired, he called Schein to tell him he couldn't turn on at his place or anywhere else they were together and Schein took the pledge, which accounted for why he was wrecked now. He always turned on before he came over.

Katz really wanted to watch James but he couldn't keep Schein from babbling over the music. Every song spurred another story, another giggling breakdown. When his elephantine version of the Camel Walk blocked the screen, Katz had enough. He pushed him on to the sofa and smacked the set off.

"You happy now?" he asked him. "Go ahead, Dumbo, you're the whole show. Dance."

Schein rolled over onto his back, laughing too hard to catch his breath.

"Hey, man," he finally wheezed out, "you used to be a lot more fun before you became a pig."

"Don't start this again, please?," Katz said.

Schein waved a hand at him.

"No problem. I promise. It was just a joke, man."

Then, after a beat, he snorted as loud as he could as hard as he could as fast as he could until he cracked himself up again.

Katz took him in, sprawled out on the sofa, arm over his eyes, laughing like a maniac, chest heaving, sweat staining the pits of his dingy gray GWU T-shirt, a fat stoned retard if there ever was one. He burst out laughing himself, sending Schein off into yet another jag of hysterics, moaning, crying, slapping the sofa with his free hand. Katz buried his head in the green shag just below him, bursting into gales of laughter every time he tried to stop. It was another two minutes before they could both get their breath.

"Yo, man," Schein finally croaked, "you give any more thought to Proxy Pickets?"

Katz flopped on to his back.

"Forget it, Schein. Like Roy Orbison said, 'It's Over',"

"It's still a great idea, man, even better now."

It was a great idea and it was Schein's but Katz got the glory for it.

One night senior year, the two of them and Weiss met at Luigi's for pizza. Their pot-fueled conversation turned to the war and a protest rally coming up at the White House.

"My sister's dying to come down for it," Weiss said, "but she can't afford it."

"How much does it cost to come down from Great Neck?" Schein asked.

"She's not in Great Neck anymore," Weiss said. "She goes to Oberlin, out in Ohio. There's no way she can get here."

Katz saw that far away look in Schein's eyes, the kind that usually preceded a proclamation like "It all fits, man!" or "Vanilla Fudge is the best band ever!"

This time he said "You know what we should do?" He put his slice down and stared right at Katz.

"Uh oh," Katz said, "stand back. If it's bigger than pizza, it's got to be huge."

"We should rent people out to march or picket or do whatever anyone wants them to do in D.C."

"I don't get it," Weiss said.

"Okay," Schein went on, "so take this thing at the White House. Let's say there's hundreds or thousands of people like your sister who can't afford to come, but still want to make sure their voices are heard. We get people to march for them."

"How do we do that?" Katz asked.

"I don't know. We put an ad in the paper or something."

"You know how much it costs to put an ad in the Post or the Star?" Schein asked.

"Maybe we do it in the Hatchet," -- the GW student paper -- "it doesn't matter. It's a great idea."

"It is," Weiss said. "We could send out letters too."

"Right," Schein said, "like to businesses or unions or anyone else who wants to put people in the streets down here. We could set rates like fifty bucks an hour for fifty people, a hundred bucks for a hundred --"

"More if you want people in suits," Weiss said.

"Right," Schein said. "This is a great idea! I had a great idea!"

Katz wasn't so sure but a few days later, Weiss got them back together at his place.

"Okay, so check this out," he said. "I got a law firm on M Street to let me use a typewriter and a mimeo machine to print up flyers."

"No way," Katz said. "How'd that happen?"

"My brother works there."

"For free?" Schein asked.

"We have to pay for the paper and the mimeo stuff. And, the Hatchet will run an ad for five bucks, or ten, depending on how big it is. Then we have to buy envelopes and stamps and get a post office box."

"For what?" Katz asked.

"For all the letters that we're going to get," Weiss said, "of course."

"That's more money," Schein said. "Why don't we just use one of our own addresses?"

"No one's going to take us seriously if the return address is Andy Scheingold, number 406, 2424 Pennsylvania Avenue," Weiss said.

"Then we come up with a name," Schein said.

"Okay, what's the name?" Katz asked.

It only took Schein a second.

"Proxy Pickets, man. How's that? Proxy Pickets! That's the name, man. I came up with a great name!"

And so Proxy Pickets was born. But when Weiss asked them for fifty bucks each to make it happen, Schein begged off.

"You cheap bastard!" Katz said. "This was your idea! And you make more money than all of us."

"This is not a good time for me to be layin' out more money," Schein said.

"What do you mean?" Katz asked.

"I got a few debts to settle first."

"For grass?" Weiss asked.

"Some, but more for the book."

"What book costs so much money?" Weiss asked.

"Not a book, jagoff, a bookie," Schein said.

Katz knew who he was talking about, a little troll of a guy named Woody who hung around the Red Lion Inn on I St.

"Schein, it's just fifty bucks," he said.

"Can't do it, man."

"Even if it's going to cost me seventy-five if you don't?"

"I can't man. I just can't. Sorry."

So Schein was out but Katz and Weiss were in. Weiss placed the ad and sent out flyers to every newspaper and magazine in town. A week or so later, he called Katz.

"Are you ready for this, man? Time magazine just called me."

"What? Why?"

"Proxy Pickets!"

"Are you shitting me?"

"I shit you not. They want to do an article on us -- and take a picture!"

"Get out of here!"

"I'm not messin' with you, man. I swear to God!"

The next week, Katz and Weiss beamed out from the People column in Time right above a story all about Schein's brilliant idea. They never got a whiff of business, but now that his finances were back in order, Schein kept pushing Katz to take another shot at it.

"Our timing was off, man, that's all. We were ahead of our time. You see this shit going on in Berkeley and Columbia. We could have a piece of that action. Anti-war business is going to be huge."

Katz had never thought about it that way. Proxy Pickets was a lark to him, not a business. Until last summer, he never really thought much about the war at all. But taking his mother shopping at Two Guys one morning, he saw Pat Ryder, one of the best running backs on his high school football team, roll up an aisle to greet him, in a wheelchair, paralyzed from the waist down. He told Katz how he got shot through the spine in some place he couldn't pronounce near Cambodia, how good he was doing, and how he still backed the war, but Katz didn't hear any of it. All he knew was this kid he played football with would never walk again. The moment they shook hands goodbye, he wanted the war to stop with all his might.

It liberated him. For the first time in his life, he had a cause worth caring about, fighting for, something bigger than himself. Now he was a rebel, willing to stand up for what he believed. He liked feeling virtuous and he liked how it made Lisa feel about him even more. They made love more often and wilder than ever before. The condom was still part of the act but getting to it was a lot more fun.

Katz kept his no-weed pledge every day, except one: October 21, 1967, the day thousands of protesters came from all over the country to rally at the Lincoln Memorial then march to the Pentagon to protest the war.

The march was planned to be the crowning event of a week of anti-war rallies across the country. The National Mobilization Committee to End the War in Vietnam organized it but Abbie Hoffman and Jerry Rubin stole the spotlight by promising that they and their Yippie followers would exorcise the Pentagon, then levitate it.

It was bad enough that he couldn't march because, like every other cop in the city, he'd be on duty. It was even worse that he might have to do something to stop it, maybe even throw gas or swing a baton at people he knew. But the worst was what drove him to get high even before the sun came up.

A couple of days earlier, Schein called him to ask if he and Lisa had room for a cousin of his from the University of Michigan who was coming to town with a "few of his friends".

"How many friends are we talking about?"

"I don't know for sure. Just a couple, I think."

"Okay, but they'll have to sleep on the sofa or the floor in the living room."

"You're great, man. I'll let him know. His name's Charlie, Charlie Friedman."

"Tell him I'll leave the key at the desk so he doesn't wake us up if they get in late."

"Solid, man. I appreciate it."

Friday night the 20th, he and Lisa walked up Pennsylvania Avenue for some veal parmigiana at Morocco's and a Marx Brothers double feature at the Circle. Coming back up the stairs a little after eleven, they heard a welter of noise from above.

"Somebody's having a party," Lisa said.

He pushed the door open at two.

"Sounds like we are," he said.

The babble of chatter was deafening. Smoke filled the landing, a thick mix of pot, tobacco, and odors he couldn't place flowing out the open doorway of their apartment. Katz picked out Otis Redding's "Shake" threading through the noise. That better not be my "Otis Blue," he thought.

He put a hand on Lisa's shoulder to keep her where she was, then walked through the door to see a crowd of people he did not know eating their food, drinking their beer, listening to their stereo. Everyone sprawled over every chair, the sofa, the carpet, the kitchen floor. Katz saw a frizzy-haired redhead, probably a girl, laying across their dining room table chatting with a guy on the toilet across the hallway.

"Make yourselves at home!" he hollered but no one turned a head in his direction.

He pushed his way back to the record player on the wall unit. The plexiglas cover was gone and "Otis Blue" spun naked on the turntable, a full ash tray and a half-full quart of National Bohemian vibrating on the shelf just above. Nothing could have pissed him off more. He gently lifted the needle off the record and parked it in its holder. That got their attention.

"Hey, man!," someone yelled. "Don't kill the music!"

"Excuse me!," Katz yelled back. "I live here. Who the hell are you?"

From the sofa across from him, a guy with bushy black hair said "Cool it, man. Andy said we could stay here."

"Andy?" Katz said. "Who the fuck is Andy?"

"Andy Scheingold, man, my cousin. He said he was your best friend. 'Course he also said you were cool so maybe he got that wrong too."

Laughter rippled across the group. Katz flushed but struggled to stay calm.

"You're Charlie?"

"I am, but my friends call me Chuck. You can call me Charlie."

"He told me you were bringing a few friends down from Michigan, not a few hundred."

"Hey, man, there's only thirty-three of us," Charlie said. "We'll be gone tomorrow, I promise. Now put the music back on, please. Pretty please?"

"Sorry, man. The party's over. My wife and I need to get some sleep. You want to stay, you keep it down. You want to have a party, you go somewhere else, okay?"

When he pointed to Lisa, Charlie and everyone else turned to see her cowering in her own doorway. He looked back at Katz with a hard stare but said "You're the boss, man. We'll behave." He held up a Boy Scout salute. "I promise. Cross my heart."

Katz took his measure. The guy looked taller than him, in shape, but he had no doubt he could kick his ass. He leveled his right index finger at him.

"If things get out of hand, you're the guy I'm gonna look for. You got that?"

An "Ooh" rippled through the room. Charlie said "No problem, hard guy. I'll be right here."

They locked eyes until Katz turned to make his way back to Lisa. He took her hand and led her to their bedroom. When he flicked on the light, he watched a tangle-haired skinny guy roll off a girl in their bed. A couple on the floor writhed in a sleeping bag.

"That's my fucking bed!" he yelled at the skinny guy staring bug-eyed back at him. "Get the fuck out of my fucking bed!"

The girl grabbed a shirt from under the sheets and held it to her chest as she dashed past them, the guy just behind, muttering apologies between giggles. The guy on the floor took his time wrapping the sleeping bag around his long-limbed blonde friend and strode out behind her, dick still erect in his boxers. He threw Katz a salute as he went out the door. Katz slammed the door behind him, muffling the roar of laughter from the living room.

He reached for Lisa but she didn't reach back. She hugged herself, shook, gulped for air.

"Lisa, honey, are you okay?"

"I can't stay here tonight, with them," she waved at the door. "With this!" She waved at the bed. "God, I'm going to be sick."

He moved to hold her but she pulled back.

"No," she said. "No!"

He held his hands up.

"Okay, do you want to go upstairs and stay with Mike and Anne? I'll walk you up there."

"Just get me to the door. I'll go up myself."

"Why are you freaking out?"

"Why am I freaking out? Are you serious? You let these people in here!"

"It's not my fault. You know what Schein told me –"

"I hate him. I hate that stupid fat bastard!"

Katz sensed it was time to end the conversation.

"Okay, okay. I'll get you out to the landing. Do you want to take some clothes or –"

"No. I just want to go. Now."

She stepped back so he could open the door for her. He pushed it open and followed her out. The conversation in the room stopped dead. He felt everyone's eyes follow them across the floor. She kept her eyes on the floor all the way to the landing. He sped up to open the door to the stairwell but she sped up too and pushed it open herself, then scuttled up the stairs. He waited till he heard her smack the door open on three, then turned and marched back through the door to their unit. His whole body was clenched, waiting, praying for someone to say something to send him over the edge. But they must have sensed that too. Everyone, even Charlie, kept their mouths shut as they watched him stride back to the bedroom.

Too many thoughts crashed into each other to let him sleep. Finally, at 4:15, he got out of bed and quietly popped the bedroom door open. He heard nothing but snores so decided to get into his uniform and out the door to avoid a hassle he didn't need. He tiptoed around and through the bodies sleeping everywhere in front of him.

Two steps from the door, he thought he had made it. But from over his shoulder, he heard a man's voice sing out.

"Something happenin' here.

"What it is ain't exactly clear."

Katz spun to face the room.

"Who the fuck is singing?" he screamed.

"There's a man with a gun over there,

"Tellin' me I got to beware."

"Show yourself, you fuckhead!"

Charlie slowly rose from the floor at the foot of the sofa to his left, softly clapping and swaying and crooning to him.

"I think it's time we stopped, children, what's that sound?

"Everybody look what's goin' down."

Katz ran right at him. He felt his left boot kick someone somewhere soft. It didn't slow him down. Charlie covered up but when Katz slammed a right fist into his ear, he came up swinging. Katz didn't feel a thing. He moved closer to him where he could get in a good shot but Charlie couldn't. He backed him up with a hard right uppercut to the chin, then grabbed the collar of his T-shirt with both hands and dug his elbows into his ribs, lifting him off the ground. Charlie pried at his hands.

"Put me down, you fucking lunatic!" he shrieked.

Whoever was under and around them scurried for the other side of the room. Katz twisted Charlie to the left, carried him two full strides, and slammed him against the wall next to the door.

A guy yelled "This is fucking police brutality!"

Katz grabbed Charlie's throat with his left hand and held his right fist up where Charlie could get a good look at it.

"You fuck with me in my own house, you fucking bastard?" Katz seethed at him.

"Okay, man," Charlie rasped. "I'm sorry, okay?"

"Get off him, man!" someone yelled. "Get his fucking badge number, Charlie!"

Katz pressed his hand tighter around Charlie's neck and turned to face the crowd. He locked eyes with the tangle-haired guy holding his girlfriend tight to him. She sobbed into his chest. He scanned the room, looking for someone who wasn't scared to death of him, who understood his anger, who knew what it was like to be on the other side. But all he saw was fear and all he heard were sobs.

He turned back to Charlie, sweating and red, his hands up against the wall. His voice came out a tiny weak whine.

" I didn't mean anything, man. I'm sorry, I'm sorry."

Katz suddenly felt tiny and weak himself. He dropped his hand from Charlie's throat and walked out the door. He drove his squad car to Schein's place off Dupont Circle. It wasn't even five o'clock but the lights were on in the townhouse basement he shared with about a million roaches. Katz saw every one of them the last time he came and Schein flipped on the light. He swore he would never come back but this time was different.

Even before he knocked on the door, Schein threw it open.

"What the fuck, man?" he said. "My cousin says you just about killed him!"

"Where's your fucking grass?," Katz said.

Schein went as wide-eyed as the kid in his bed.

"You busting me?", he asked.

"No, man, I want to smoke it and get as stoned as I possibly can."

Schein asked no more questions. The two of them sucked down a pipe each. When Katz felt the egg break over his head, he knew it was time to go.

"See you at the Memorial," he said to Schein and strolled back to his cruiser, enjoying the beautiful sunrise streaking the sky red, brown, orange, gold, and purple.

"'For purple mountains' majesties, above the fruited plain'!," he sang out.

It was the only way he got through the day.

14

Lisa was already so pissed at him when he told her no, he still hadn't let GW know he was coming in September that he figured he had nothing to lose when he told her he was spending his first day off since the riots driving up to Baltimore. He couldn't stop replaying the conversation all the way up the Parkway.

"What are you waiting for, Jake?"

"I just want to make sure we have the money. We haven't saved nearly enough yet."

She waved the letter at him.

"They don't want it all now, just five hundred dollars! We've put away a lot more than that already."

"That's just the deposit. We're going to have to come up with three years of tuition, maybe more."

"Jake, this is just so much b.s. I'm working – and I'm going to keep working. You're working full time for another, what, five months? You can get loans, you can work summers. We've worked it out. What is the problem?"

"What if you have to stop working?"

"Here we go again with the baby, right? We're using rubbers, honey, and we're going to keep using rubbers, okay? Get it through your head -- I'm not having a baby!"

There were a lot of things Katz could've said then.

That he hated the damn rubbers because they killed the pleasure.

That he wanted to get her pregnant because then he'd have to keep working to support the baby.

That he had to stay at MPD, that he wanted to stay.

But he didn't say any of that.

He said "Fine. You're right. I'm sorry. I'll send them the check, I promise."

Then he told her he was going to Baltimore.

A funky beat on a high-hat cymbal got his attention. He turned up the radio. "I Heard It Through the Grapevine". Gladys Knight and the Pips. He pictured them gliding through their steps at the Howard. So slick, so effortless. He loved that song. He wanted to be a Pip -- or a Jack or a Tempt or a Miracle, it didn't really matter. He'd sell his soul to have the grace of any of them for five minutes.

Then he pictured Brenda Queen. Not in her spangled dress but naked on that gurney, all her sordid secrets bare to the world. What secrets was Gladys Knight hiding? It made him sick to even think that. He flicked the radio off.

Katz found his way to Old York Road and pulled out the piece of paper where he'd written Albert Reynolds' office address. He found a parking space just up the block and walked back down to the building bearing the number. He looked at his watch. Five-thirty. Right on time. He walked in through the open door. No one at the reception desk.

"Hello," he called out to the hallway past the desk. No answer, just the faint sound of a radio. He walked around the desk and down the hall in the direction of the sound. He poked his head into open doorways on each side of the hall. No one around.   He heard music faintly playing behind the closed door at the end of the hall. He rapped a little skip knock on the door.

"Mr. Reynolds? Jake Katz. With the DC police?"

No answer. He pushed the door but it wouldn't open all the way. He pushed harder but it wasn't moving. He squeezed his head through the opening and looked down at a dead man.

He ran back to the reception desk and dialed 0 on the phone.

"Operator, I need the police. There's a dead body at 2404 Old York Road!"

He was only outside for five minutes before the cruiser pulled up. A tall white man in a dark blue pinstriped suit unfolded from the passenger seat. Katz came down the walkway to meet him. He tried to think who he looked like. Craggy face, cleft chin, wavy brown hair fading gray. Some movie star, he couldn't remember his name.

"Hi. Jake Katz, DC Police."

"Ted Harris. Detective, Baltimore PD." He looked Katz' civilian duds up and down. "You here on business or --?"

"Business. I had an appointment with Mr. Reynolds about Brenda Queen's death at the Howard."

"Who?" Harris asked. "Where?"

"Sorry. Brenda Queen was a singer, a soul singer. She was shot on stage at the Howard Theatre in DC, during the riots."

"Okay. What's this Reynolds got to do with that?"

"He was her accountant. One of the witnesses I talked to thought he might be able to help provide some information about who might have wanted to kill her."

Harris nodded.

"So you're a detective?"

"No, a patrolman." He started to give him the whole story but the quizzical look on Harris' face made him cut it short. "I'm just trying to help out."

The cop who parked the car up the street joined them. Harris introduced them, then gestured to Katz to lead them in. He walked them back to the door to Reynolds' office and pointed down through the opening. Harris knelt to take a look, then called over his shoulder.

"Johnny, see if you can get in from the back."

Johnny ran back up the hallway and ducked out the door to the right.

Harris studied the room a little more but said nothing. He stood up and waited for Johnny. In a few seconds, they heard him call out.

"There's a back door. It was open. Come down the walk."

Katz followed Harris down the pebbled path along the building into an alley running the length of the block. They went up the single step at the rear of the building and into Reynolds' office.

Reynolds lay directly across the room from them, face down. His left side was hard up against the door, his legs splayed in their direction, like a running back in mid-stride.

A desk faced them just to the left of the door. Katz followed Harris around the side farthest away from the body. A deep drawer was pulled all the way out, with files strewn across the carpet. The long middle drawer was open too. The desktop was almost bare. Harris pulled a pair of thin black gloves from his inside suit pocket and slid them on before approaching Reynolds. He knelt down and reached across the body, patting his left rear pants pocket, then his right. He pulled him by the left shoulder, rolling him over on his back. The front of his shirt was stained red with the blood still oozing from the center of his chest.

"He hasn't been dead long," Harris said. He pulled the glove off his right hand and touched the back of his palm to Reynolds' forehead. "Cool, not cold."

He slid the glove back on and reached into the inside pockets of the dead man's suit jacket, then patted his front pants pockets.

"No wallet, no check book," he called over his shoulder to Johnny, then stood up and smoothed the wrinkles from his pants. Katz came to his side to look at the body.

"If it helps," he said, "I came here to ask him about whether Brenda Queen's husband might have been skimming money or making him cook the books some way."

"It doesn't," Harris said.

"Doesn't what?" Katz asked.

"Help."

Katz waited for more but Harris wasn't giving it, so he asked.

"You're sure?"

Harris looked at Katz with the air of a man who was being forced to explain the obvious to an imbecile, then perched himself on the corner of the desk so he could at least be comfortable doing it.

"Patrolman, this is a burglary gone bad."

Katz had to admit it looked that way, but what if it did because Walker Thomas wanted it to look that way? What if he came to get the files that would incriminate him, then set it up to look like a burglary? Why was Harris as sure as Wallace that there wasn't more here than met the eye?

"I understand that's what it looks like, I do," he said. " But couldn't it be possible that somebody set it up to look that way?"

"I'm going to let you in on a trick of the trade, officer. Ninety-nine point ninety-nine percent of the time, whatever the evidence says something looks like, that's what it is."

Katz had heard that before but decided not to fight about it this time. He just nodded.

"So this is what the evidence looks like here. We've got an entry through a rear door into the office of an accountant. The accountant tried to get out through the front door but he was stabbed in the chest. His wallet, maybe a checkbook are missing, and anything that was on his desk that might have looked like it was worth anything is gone too. To me, that points to something that started out a burglary and ended up a murder."

Katz had to admit it looked like that to him too -- except for the radio. Why wouldn't a burglar take that?

"Probably too big to carry," Harris said.

He must have flicked his eyes up to the shelf and Harris caught it. He was good. Maybe that's why he decided not to put up a fight this time.

It wasn't till he was halfway back down the Parkway that another reason why occurred to him. He took a hard look at himself in the mirror, then turned away, trying to ignore the flush scalding his cheeks.

15

Katz took his time down the steps to the basement and looked through the window of the first door on the right. About twenty rows of metal folding chairs ran from the back to the desk Jarvie perched on at the front of the room. A Lieutenant leaving the room held the door open for him so he had no choice but to go in. He ducked into the seat closest to the door and surveyed the crowd. Most of the top brass was down front – Chief Wilson, Deputy Pine, a lot of captains and commanders – but he didn't see one other street cop. He was just about to duck back out when Jarvie threw him a salute.

"Patrolman, good to see you here."

Too late now. He forced a grin and saluted back.

Every month or so, Jarvie posted a notice inviting all hands to attend a briefing at headquarters on the latest court cases affecting the way the department went about its business. Katz thought he might take one in just to see if he and law school really were meant for each other.

He thought back to the constitutional law course he took with Professor Morgan his junior year. Morgan was a courtly Southerner who smoked a pipe in class and made his students confront the logic, and sometimes the illogic, underlying not only the law but their own beliefs. Katz got clammy all over again reliving their "debate" about why eighteen-year-olds should be able to vote. He winced hearing himself again, so assertive, so sure.

"If you're old enough to fight in a war, you're old enough to vote."

The murmur of approval all around buoyed him up. Morgan waited for it to dissipate, then pointed his pipe stem at him.

"I hear that all the time -- and I never understand it. What on earth does one thing have to do with the other? Can you explain to me what the country's need for soldiers has to do with who should choose its leaders? Why does being physically fit enough for military service have anything to do with whether someone has the mental capacity to cast a thoughtful vote? If we needed to induct twelve-year-olds into the army, does that mean they should have the right to vote too?"

He put the pipe back in his mouth and stared intently at Katz, who had no answer or even the capacity to answer any of that. After what seemed an eternity, Morgan released a puff of smoke and turned his gaze to the class at large.

"Of course, I pose these simply as rhetorical questions."

That trial by fire was what sparked his interest in law school in the first place. He thought he'd see if Jarvie's briefings might reignite it.

"Happy May Day, everyone," Jarvie said. "It's Law Day too, so be sure to call your lawyer today and tell him how much you love him."

He handed a sheaf of mimeo sheets to the captain in front of him who passed them down the aisle and up over his shoulder. Katz saw it was a summary of a court decision named Harris v. United States.

"Okay. Today, we're going to talk about Harris v. U.S., a case the Supreme Court decided last month that started with an arrest right here in D.C. Anybody remember Mr. James H. Harris?"

No response.

"I'm not surprised. It was just a run of the mill robbery case. But it did present an issue that was important to the Court and its decision is going to be important to you too."

107

"Oh, Jesus, here we go again," someone said. Jarvie held up his hand to quiet the snorts and chuckles that followed.

"Hold on now. You just might be surprised by this one. It seems that someone saw Mr. Harris' car leaving the scene of the crime. We traced it to his address and arrested him when he came out and got into it. Then we took the car to the impound lot to hold as evidence. When it got there, an officer went through it per the regs, which means, in case you never pulled this duty, he searched the vehicle, removed all the valuables, and tied a note to the steering wheel saying when and how it got there.

"Now this particular night, it was raining, so, being a good guy, of course, the cop goes around the car to roll up all the windows. When he opens the passenger door, he looks down and, lo and behold, he sees a registration card on the metal strip the door closes over. He picks it up and sees Mr. Harris' name on there so he takes it in to him and ask him how it got there. Mr. Harris, big surprise, says he has no idea. Our guy holds on to it and adds it to the evidence against Mr. Harris, who is subsequently convicted.

"So, the question that Mr. Harris' lawyer raised – Paul Weinstein, by the way, a very good guy and a very good lawyer – was whether that was unconstitutional under the Fourth Amendment to the Constitution, which – anyone?"

"Prohibits unreasonable searches and seizures," a captain in front of Katz said.

"Very good. You go to the head of the class. Correct, prohibits unreasonable searches and seizures. So, did it? Was this an unreasonable search and seizure?"

"I don't think so," Deputy Pine said, "but I'll bet those jackoffs did."

Jarvie waited for the laughter to die down.

"Now I told you you'd be surprised. They actually found, first, that there wasn't really even a search. The cop was just trying to protect the car when he came across the card, not search it. Then they said that he had every right to seize the card because it came into plain view while he was doing his permissible activities. So there you go. Conviction upheld. Bad guy goes to jail."

Deputy Pine turned in his seat to face the group.

"So that's the rule around here from now on, okay? No one searches a car until it starts raining, then everything's fair game."

Katz laughed along with the rest of them, then made himself read through the opinion. When he finished, he had more questions than answers, like when was a search not a search? If MPD didn't have that reg and the cop was just trying to protect the car because he was such a good guy, would that have been unconstitutional? Did what the cop intended really determine if a search was constitutional or not? Then what would keep him from lying about why he did what he did, if that was the only way to make the arrest stick? Most importantly, did he want to dedicate his life to asking these kinds of questions? Jarvie did but he quit. Maybe he'd be a good guy to talk to.

He felt a large hand squeeze his shoulder. He looked up to see Jarvie smiling down at him.

"Thanks for coming. You guys on the street are the ones who really need this training but you're the first one who ever showed up. I appreciate it."

"Thank you, Sarge. It was great, really interesting."

"Well, come again – and bring your buddies."

He patted him on the shoulder and went out the door. Before he could stop himself, Katz followed and caught up with him.

"Actually, I had another reason for coming."

"Oh, yeah. What's that?"

"I'm thinking of going to law school."

"Ah, I see." Jarvie stopped and looked at his watch. "Got any lunch plans?"

"No."

"Let's talk about it at A.V. Meet you there at noon."

16

One short block from the station, A.V. Ristorante was the primo perk of working in the 1st. For four years, no issue divided Katz and his GW cronies more than whether A.V. or Luigi's served the best pizza in town. Katz came down firmly on the A.V. side. Luigi's was a lot closer to campus, but the trek to 6th and New York made the payoff at A.V.'s even tastier.

Gus grabbed Jarvie's hands in his own, then wrapped a bear arm around his shoulders.

"Mio avvocato. How've you been?"

"Great, Gus, just great."

"Come, I give you the best seat in the house."

He led them through a maze of flaming red rooms to a table big enough for six that filled the wall between the kitchen and the phone booth.

"Signor," Gus said to Jake, "what can I get you from the bar?"

"Get whatever you like," Jarvie said. "The wine comes in juice glasses. I'll never tell."

"Coke's good," Jake said.

"The usual," Jarvie said.

Gus gave him a thumbs up and left them alone.

"He loves you," Jake said. Jarvie shrugged.

"I used to be his lawyer. I got some drunks off his back, then he started feeding me some business problems, taxes, a lot of day-to-day stuff that helped pay the rent. Good guy, good client."

Gus came back with Jake's Coke and a glass of fizzy water.

"And to eat?"

Jarvie looked at Katz.

"White pizza?"

"You bet."

"Anchovies?"

"Yes sir."

Jarvie looked up at Gus. "White pizza, anchovies, grande."

When Gus left, Katz pointed at Jarvie's glass. "That's the usual?"

"Didn't used to be. Is now. Cheers."

They clinked glasses.

"I'll give you the Reader's Digest version," Jarvie said. "I really liked being a lawyer. I liked the work, loved the money, really, really loved beating the other side into the ground every way I could. So what if it turned me into a bigger prick than my wife could stand, my kids could stand, any of my partners could stand? Tough shit. I could stand me just fine. Went on like that for years. Then, one day, out of nowhere, after it was way, way, too late to save anything that really meant anything, it hit me. A moment of clarity. Sitting straight up in bed, sweat streaming down my face, my chest. October 13, 1960. 3:14 in the morning. Never forget it. Everything I'd done to everybody, to myself, just hit me four square, right in the kisser. Bam! I got up, went to work, quit the firm, the booze too, everything that was killing me, right on the spot. I took a little time to dry out, then I called Chief Murray about coming here and, God bless him, he didn't hold a grudge about all the guys I helped beat the rap. He jumped at it." He downed a swig of seltzer and shrugged his shoulders. "That's it. "

That amazed Katz, not just the story, but that he could share it with a total stranger.

"Shocked?" Jarvie asked. "I didn't mean to kill the conversation."

"No, no," Katz laughed. "You just poured out your life story to me and I can't even tell my wife what's on my mind."

"Okay, so tell me. What's on your mind?"

The arrival of the pizza gave him a reprieve. The garlic and oregano overwhelmed them both.

"Another masterpiece, Gus! Grazi, multi grazi."

"My pleasure, always." He made a little bow and backed away.

They each tugged a piece onto their plates, then started in with gusto.

"The best," Katz crowed.

Jarvie nodded and finished his bite.

"So you want to go to law school. I know that much."

"Yeah. I got accepted at GW last year but I didn't have the money to start, so they're holding my place."

"So that's why you came to my little session this morning? To give it a test drive?"

"Yeah. Sorry."

"So, did you withdraw your application yet?"

Katz laughed. "No, it was really interesting. Made me think."

"About what?"

Katz laid out the questions that ran through his mind reading the case. Jarvie nodded his approval.

"You know what they call that?"

"No."

"Thinking like a lawyer."

Katz tugged another piece of pizza free and wondered whether he was thinking like a lawyer about Brenda Queen too.

"Sarge, do you know about the Brenda Queen case, the singer who was shot up at the Howard?"

"Yeah, sure. Are you working on that?"

"Kind of. I'm trying to help the detective on it but he doesn't want any help, at least mine."

"Why?"

Katz laid that out for him too and waited for Jarvie to finish sliding down a roll of crust and cheese.

"Who's the detective?"

"Wallace, from the 13th."

"Well, that explains a lot."

He wiped a napkin across his mouth and drained his seltzer.

"First of all, 'Tom' is probably not the name he would've picked for himself if he knew he was going to be a cop."

Katz got the reference. He remembered some of the militant Negroes calling Martin Luther King an Uncle Tom.

"But more important, Tom Wallace is a very good detective and he was a very good plainclothesman before that, for a long time, too long a time, and we both know why."

Katz didn't so he asked why.

"I don't know the ins and outs of what happened to him specifically but what I do know is the Department's gearing up for a major lawsuit from the black guys on the force claiming MPD's keeping 'em down, and probably another one from the black guys who never made it on, claiming we're keeping them out. I can only imagine what it's like to stand in his shoes but if I was him and whitey was trying to cut the rungs in front of me all the way up the ladder, I'd be worried too if some white boy coming up from behind said he was here to help me."

"Okay, I get all that, but leave me out of it. I talked to the manager at the Howard and one of the backup singers and I've already got a good list of people who had all kinds of reasons to want her dead. He's a detective. He should be trailing every lead, shouldn't he?"

"I told you you were thinking like a lawyer, right?"

"Yeah."

"Well, he's thinking like a cop. He's looking for the evidence to point him in the right direction, not instincts, not intuition, not maybes or maybe nots. That's how he does his job. Lawyers, they've got another job. The prosecutor needs to tell a story the jury will believe beyond a reasonable doubt, so he needs reasons, motives, all that, to make it convincing. Defense counsel's job is to plant doubt, reasonable or unreasonable, about every part of the story, invent reasons for why something might have happened, who else might have done the deed, make the jury think there's something the other side isn't telling you."

"So then, what? If Wallace can't connect the dots, a murderer goes free?"

Jarvie shook his head.

"Let him come to it in his own way. Now that he's got the autopsy results, he's got a reason other than you to start thinking it might be murder."

That made sense to Katz but waiting wasn't his strong suit.

"So I just sit and hope he finds his way?"

"No, you should keep on keeping on. Isn't that what they say these days? If you come across something, you let him know. He'll do what's right. Eventually."

Katz pushed away his plate. Jarvie got the message. He put his big hand on Katz' arm and leaned in close to talk to him.

"Son, that lady's dead and she's going to be dead tomorrow and forever after. Rushing Wallace isn't going to bring her back. Just give him time to do what's right. You just might be surprised how everything turns out."

115

17

She liked hearing that he talked to Jarvie about being a lawyer.

She liked that he stopped to buy her a spray of spring flowers before he came home.

She let him know how much she liked him in the way he always appreciated.

He put the TV on for some light and turned the volume off, then slid under the sheets and pulled her to him. The Smothers Brothers sang silently at the foot of the bed. She rubbed his tummy and he began to rise to the occasion.

"I can't see them," she cooed. "Something's in the way."

"What could it be?" he asked.

She reached down and pulled him up and out from under the sheets.

"Well, looky here," she said, then slid down his chest and across his stomach, kissing and nibbling him all the way down, then all the way up. She turned so he could see her, licking him softly and so sweetly all the while.

"Don't watch me, honey," she whispered. "Watch Tommy. I'll watch Dickie."

He tried but it was hard and harder every time she inhaled him, licked him, inhaled him again --

He tickled her under the chin.

"Come up here."

She did as she was told, pressing down onto him all the way up. He reached between her legs and tickled her. She lifted herself off his stomach and let him slide a finger inside, then two. She swayed up and back in time to his motion. Sweat trickled down her breasts. His fingers grew moist. He pushed his dick up against her and lifted her so he could guide himself in.

She bent down to kiss him, tickling his chest with her tits, then slid up and reached into the drawer of the nightstand and plucked out a Trojan.

"Come on," he cooed, "just this once. Wouldn't it feel good?"

She bit the corner, ripped the foil, and slid the rubber out.

He could feel himself losing it. Until she pushed herself back down and sucked him harder this time while her fingers danced up and down his shaft, under his balls, and back up again. Then she slid the bag over him. He filled it up, then filled her. He reached for her breasts and she squeezed his hands to them. They pushed into each other hard and fast until she moaned and he couldn't hold it back any more and they burst together.

When they finally came to rest, she collapsed into his waiting arms. They breathed in time. He panted quicker just to make her laugh and she did.

"I love you," she whispered, hoping that was all they'd need.

"I love you," he whispered back, worried that wasn't enough.

18

Floyd begged to come too so they headed for the cruiser together. Katz pulled out of the parking lot and headed up 6th bound for the Howard.

Floyd pointed to the radio.

"No, you," Katz said. "Go ahead."

"Again? What's the deal?"

"Nothing. Put on anything you want."

Floyd punched up WEAM. Bobby Goldsboro. "Honey, I miss you and I'm –"

"Anything but that."

Floyd twirled to WPGC. The Monkees. "Valerie."

Floyd wailed along on the chorus but Katz didn't hear him. He was looking at all the empty storefronts lining both sides of the street. He knew the "We Cheat You Right" store was around here but he couldn't find a window much less the sign. A month after the riot, no one was back in business. Seven o'clock at night, no one was on the street, black or white.

He slid into a parking space at the corner of T.

"There she is."

Floyd turned to see the Howard for the first time. It looked to Katz like it always did, a rundown unassuming little building that never gave a hint of the excitement it held inside. The glass showcases touting the new shows were all intact.

"Looks like they left it alone," Floyd said.

Katz led him to the front doors. He saw no one in the lobby but gave the door a pull anyway. It opened. They walked up into the theatre. Floyd took it all in.

"Jesus!," he said. "This place is a dump!"

Katz had to agree. Soda cups, popcorn bags, candy boxes, and cigarette packs cluttered the aisle in front of them.

Floyd kicked a beer bottle, sending it skittering and clanging under a row of seats. A sleeping bag flopped over the seats to their right. The reek of the place, a thick mix of tobacco, booze, ammonia, and sweat, overwhelmed them. The dark bare stage added to the sense of decay.

They heard a door close down to the left and turned to see a slight black man limp slowly up the aisle. Even Em Crowe looked worse for wear, his shoulders bowed, his gait unsteady. Did all this happen in a month, Katz wondered, or was he just too dazzled the last time he was here? Even before he reached them, Katz could smell the alcohol.

"We let ourselves in," he said. "The door was unlocked."

"So what now?," Crowe said. "Box office opens in five minutes."

Katz gave him the quick recap of his conversation with Edward, then finding Reynolds dead. If Crowe was surprised, he didn't show it.

"So I'm not sure where to go next," Katz said.

"Is that my problem?," Crowe asked. He wobbled past them to the ticket booth and jerked the door open. "Your detective friend don't have any ideas?"

"If he does, he's keeping them to himself," Katz said. "Has he been back?"

Em fell into the seat behind the box office window with a loud grunt, bent down under the counter, and pulled up a beat-up blue strongbox before he answered.

"No."

"Do you know if Jerome is still around? I checked at the Whitelaw and Cecilia's and they said he wasn't there. I thought you might know –"

"I don't know and I don't want to know. Got enough problems of my own."

119

Katz watched Em spin the dials on the front of the box and pop it open. It was empty.

"Mr. Crowe, why are you here, in the booth?"

"I'm the only one left. Had to lay 'em all off, except the candy bar lady and that's only 'cause she's family. Plus, I ain't sellin' no damn candy bars."

"But I thought the Howard was different. No one touched it."

"No one did but ain't no one coming here either. You look around on your way up? Ain't nothin' open, nowhere to go, eat, drink. You get the picture?"

Katz got it.

"Leelee! Get back in there! I'll be done here in a minute."

Katz and Floyd turned to look at a heavyset girl, maybe fifteen or so, standing with her hands clasped in front of her chest. Katz remembered her from the candy counter. She opened her mouth, then thought better of it and ran back through the door.

"My niece. She's a little slow. What can I say?"

Floyd nudged Katz and tipped his head towards the sidewalk.

"Who's here tonight?" Katz asked.

"Billy Stewart. Patti LaBelle and the Bluebells. Joe Cuba. Hell of a show." Em shook his head. "Be lucky if the band shows up to see 'em."

Katz pulled his wallet out.

"Give me two. Floyd, my treat."

Floyd started to say something but Katz cut him off.

"No, I insist."

"That's seven bucks."

Em put the money in the box and ripped two ticket stubs from a roll on the counter.

"You got any other friends that might want to come up? Because there is one other thing I think you might want to check out."

"Is that right? How many friends are we talking about?"

"How about another ten?"

"I don't know if I have ten friends. How about five?"

"How 'bout six?"

Katz checked his wallet. Sixteen bucks.

"Floyd, you think you might want to treat one of your friends?"

"Hell no!"

"I'll pay you back."

"Fuckin' shakedown," Floyd muttered but he coughed up a five.

Em took the money, counted it out, pulled off six more stubs, and handed them to Katz.

"You see the paper today?"

"The Post?"

"Afro-American." He pointed to the floor. "There. Bring it up here."

Katz bent down to pick up the paper strewn at Em's feet. Em yanked off the top page and handed it to him. He pointed at a headline at the top of the page. Katz read "Stax Stars Now Sing for Warners".

"She was going to be one of 'em. There was some bad stuff brewin' between Stax and Atlantic for a long time, then Warners jumped into it. Some big legal deal about who owned the records and whatnot. Johnny B can tell you all about it."

"Who's Johnny B?"

"Fella that wrote the article. That's his thing, soul music. Writes on it every paper."

"Okay, I'll talk to him."

"Now get out of here. I gotta sell some tickets. You see anyone out there, you send 'em over, okay?"

"No problem," Katz said. He followed Floyd out the door and over to the car. They looked up and down the street. No one in sight. He knew what Em Crowe knew. This was the end of the Howard, the end of an era, the last time he would be back. They got in the car. He looked at Floyd.

"You owe me five bucks, Ikey."

Katz hung a U-turn and headed back to the station.

19

"You owe me five bucks, Ikey."

"I got you, Floyd. Bailey, give me three bucks. That's with tip."

The food at the FOP was no better than McDonald's but you couldn't beat the price. Roast beef sandwich and fries, a buck ninety-five. Soup, thirty-five cents. Ice cream, two scoops, a quarter. They'd be on the can all night but what a deal.

Bailey nodded toward a table near the door.

"You know those fuckers?" he asked Katz.

Katz turned to see three Negroes, two in uniform and Wallace, standing up to go. They all seemed to be amused. Katz caught eyes with Wallace and held his stare until the detective turned to leave, shaking his head.

"Yeah, the guy in the sport jacket," Katz said.

"What's his fuckin' problem?" Bailey asked.

"He's a detective. He thinks I'm horning in on his case, Brenda Queen."

"The coon singer? You're workin' on that?"

"A little."

"Katz loves the nigger music," Floyd said. "You should see this place where she got shot. Should be condemned."

Bailey flipped Katz his three dollars. Katz slid them to Floyd.

"I got your lunch. We're even."

He covered the bill, then followed them out the door.

"Yo! Katz!"

They all turned to see one of the Negro cops they'd just seen inside.

"The fuck's your problem, asshole?" Bailey yelled. Katz held up a hand and walked over to him.

"What is your problem, man?"

"You, man. You're my problem."

"Really? Why's that?"

"You tryin' to make detective on the back of a brother. Got it right, don't I?"

Katz glanced down at the name tag over his pocket. V. Crawford.

"Crawford, you have no idea what you're talking about."

"I know what I know. Little b'wana gonna show the natives how it's done, right?"

"Did Wallace put you up to this?"

"Why'd you pick one of his cases, man? Did Layton or Pine put you up to that? Find a way to fuck the colored boy? Too many of us movin' up? That it?"

Katz could feel Floyd and Bailey at his back.

"Aw, now here come the other crackers to protect you from the Ne-gro. You better back off, man. Before you get backed off."

Bailey yelled something at him as he turned to walk away but Katz couldn't hear it over the pounding of his heart.

20

Katz was the first to arrive and the place was nearly empty so he grabbed a table close to the stage. A waitress wearing nothing above the belt but red star-shaped pasties came by right away.

"What'll it be?"

He wanted to wait for his pals but he remembered the first time he came to Casino Royale his freshman year, just to ogle the titties. He told the waitress he didn't want anything. She told him to order or leave. He didn't need to be told again.

"How about a pitcher of Black Label?"

She disappeared and he checked his watch. Seven sharp. The place was usually packed by now. He saw Weiss back by the door and waved at him.

"Hey, man. How are you?"

"Better, now. Just got done my last final about three hours ago. What a bitch!"

The waitress came back with the pitcher and two glasses.

"You expecting more?"

"Yeah," Katz said. "Should be four or five."

"Good. I can use the company."

"Yeah, what's the story? Where is everybody?"

"Since the riots, no one's coming down here, except -
-"

He followed her eye to the table at the other end of the stage. Two portly men, probably in their sixties, flanked a beautiful dark-haired girl wrapped in a man's suit jacket.

"The guy without the coat," the waitress said, "he's a big muckety-muck in the Congress. The other guy's with him pretty much every night."

"Holy shit!" Weiss said. "That's Hambrick, my tax professor!"

"Are you kidding me?" Katz said.

"No! Oh, that's so funny. He's always making jokes about strippers."

"Like what?"

"Like," he lowered his voice into a slow Southern drawl, "'there was this one with breasts so big, her pasties were C-cup'."

"That's him," the waitress said. "Four bucks, gents."

Katz gave her a five and she left.

"'Ah knew anothah one had breasts so big, they called her the dairy queen.'"

"Wow," Katz said. "He said that in class? In front of women?"

"At least one. I remember she slammed her book shut, picked up her stuff, and walked out, right in the middle of class. Didn't faze him in the least. He just kept right on going."

Scheingold pulled up a chair.

"Yo. How goes it?"

"Yo. Where's everyone else?" Katz asked.

"They said they'd be here, but maybe they got spooked. Sorry. Bad joke."

The waitress set down a tray with four glasses. Scheingold couldn't take his eyes off her cleavage until she turned to leave. Then he couldn't take his eyes off her ass.

"Man, I love this place," he said.

"So, you made it through," Katz said to Weiss. "Tell me about it."

"It was horrible, man, with a capital H. Don't come."

"Are you serious?"

"Shit, yes. There was nothing fun or even pleasant about it. The courses are boring, the professors can't teach,

126

and the guys I'm with are total assholes. And those are the high points."

"Terrific! Sounds great!"

"On the other hand, I'm not putting down civil insurrection every day so let's keep it in perspective."

"He likes it," Schein said. "That's fun for him."

"It's not fun. It's – exciting, it's interesting. I feel like I'm contributing something to someone, sometimes at least."

"I can safely say that I felt none of that any time this whole year. Maybe you ought to stick with it."

"Yeah, maybe," Scheingold said, "except his wife'll kill him if no one else does first."

"It's not like that," Katz said. Except it is, he thought.

"When do you have to let them know if you're coming?"

"What's today?"

"May 20th."

"I still have a while. End of July."

"Man, you've got a tough call to make. Good luck."

They caught up through dinner. Weiss was still shacked up with Anne but she was putting the squeeze on him to make her legal. Katz extolled the virtues of married life, real and imagined. Weiss was having none of it.

"Nice try, Jake, but I'm going to ride this train as long as I can. Keep my options open."

He looked at his watch. 8:15.

"Oh, shit," he said. "She's going to kill me. I told her I'd take her to the Circle tonight, celebrate my release with Harold and Maude." He got up and dug into his wallet.

Katz laughed. "Your train sounds a lot like mine, man. Come on, I'll walk you out."

Schein was shocked.

"The girls are coming out in five minutes!"

"Schein, we see naked women every day, without leaving the house," Katz said. "You coming?"

Schein looked at his watch.

"You know what? I'm going to hang around a little bit just in case anyone else decides to show up."

"Of course," Katz said. "You are such a good friend."

He walked Weiss out the door and on to 14th St. Weiss pointed at the cruiser sitting under the "No Parking" sign at the curb.

"That you?"

"Perk of the job."

"Now I see the appeal."

They said their goodbyes and Katz headed home. He had to settle for a space down the block. He took the steps to the apartment two at a time. Lisa would still be up. Maybe she wouldn't be too tired.

The door swung open before he could get his keys out. Lisa looked like hell, eyes rimmed red, hair a mess.

"Jake, you got a call tonight. It scared me to death."

He closed the door and followed her to the phone. She picked up the notepad they kept there and slapped it into his hand.

"I tried to write it all down as soon as he hung up. I was going crazy waiting for you!"

Katz tried to read what she'd written but the words jumped all over the page.

"I can't read this. What did he say?"

"He said you need to keep your nose out of where it doesn't belong and that if you didn't, he'd make sure you did 'permanently'. God, Jake, who is he? What does he want?"

"What did he sound like?"

"Like a Negro."

128

"Did he say anything else?"

She grabbed his wrists.

"'I know where you live'! God damn it, Jake, he knows where we live! How can I stay here? You're never here!"

Katz' mind reeled. Was it Wallace? Walker Thomas? Jerome Terry? Someone else?

"You can't, you can't. I know."

"Why did he call here? What does he want you to keep your nose out of?"

"I don't know."

She threw his arms down and stalked to the other side of the room, then stormed back.

"How can you not know? How many people want to kill you? Two, three, twenty?"

He reached out to hold her but she pushed him away.

"You and this fucking police job. How could you do this to me?"

He flopped into a chair and tried to think but it was too much to sort out. The only good answer was that he had no good answer.

"I'm sorry, Lisa. I never thought it would come to this. You do need to go, get out of the city. Go to your mother's. I'd die if anything ever happened to you."

She ran into the bedroom, wailing, and slammed the door behind her. He started to get up but stopped. He didn't know what to do, here or anywhere else.

21

The silence was killing him. There was nothing he could say but he had to say something.

"This is for the best," he said. "It'll only be for a while."

She kept looking for the cab. When it finally came, he reached for the suitcase but she pulled it from his hand and dragged it to the back of the car. The driver threw it in the trunk. Katz held the door open for her but she got in the other side. He bent down to give it one more try.

"Lisa, don't go like this. I'm going to wrap this thing up as soon as I can. It'll work out before September, I promise."

She stared straight ahead. The driver got in the car and turned the ignition.

"Lisa --"

"We need to go," she told the driver. "I don't want to miss this train."

The driver turned to Katz. Katz closed the door. The cab took off. He ran back to their car. He took off after them but had to stop at the light at 24th. It gave him time to realize that the best thing he could do for both of them was what he promised.

He headed for 11th and S.

22

Katz picked up a copy of the paper while the receptionist looked for Johnny B. "Negro Olympic Boycott Urged!" took up half the top fold. He remembered reading somewhere that Lew Alcindor was thinking about boycotting the Games. He skimmed through the article and got the point but, still, he thought, this is the Olympics. We need those guys.

"Officer?"

The receptionist pointed to the back of an Afro bobbing up over a room divider across the room. "That's him back there."

Katz weaved his way across the floor. Fat headphones clamped Johnny B's head, his ragged bush exploding all around them. An album cover with five or six Negro men and women standing on something concrete laid on his desk. Johnny stomped both feet on the floor and slapped his thighs in time. Katz tapped him lightly on the shoulder. When he spun around, Katz did a double take.

"You're Johnny B?"

"Kat-Man!"

He yanked off the head phones and wrapped Katz' hand in an extended soul shake.

Johnny B was John Benton, the only Negro on Katz' freshman dorm floor. He was an exotic specimen to Katz, the first black kid he ever talked to. The only other one he ever spoke to in four years at GW was a guy named Vince Gray, the first Negro to pledge a fraternity. Even though he wasn't a member, Katz took pride in the fact that it was a Jewish frat, Tau Epsilon Phi, that let him in.

It was Benton who actually introduced Katz to the Howard – the Four Tops, Martha and the Vandellas, and the Marvelettes, November '64. They even played on the same intramural basketball team, but after they moved to different dorms sophomore year, they didn't do much but wave to each other and even that stopped after a while, maybe when John joined the Black Student Union. The last time Katz saw him was at a Black Solidarity rally on campus, when he was trying to pull Marion Barry and Catfish Mayfield off each other after they started duking it on stage about who was the real community organizer in D.C.

Johnny rolled back his chair to take in the view.

"So dig you. A real live DC pig!"

"Come on, you know me better than that."

"What happened to you, man?"

Katz gave him the thirty-second summary.

"Okay, I can dig it. But, man, you gave me a nervous ten seconds there. Thought all those nickel bags caught up to me."

"And you?"

"Kind of a cool gig here. Paper comes out twice a week. I get to listen to my music and they pay me for writin' about it." He pointed to the album cover. Dance to the Music Sly & The Family Stone. "You hear these cats yet?"

"No."

"Oh, my Lord. Sit down. Check this out."

He planted Katz in the chair next to his desk and handed him one of the headphones. He moved the needle and motioned Katz to listen.

"It's called 'Higher'!" he yelled. Katz could barely grab the beat but it was a thumping piece of rock or soul or whatever it was.

Johnny B pointed at him and mouthed "'Boomalakalakalaka! Boomalakalakalaka!' along with Sly. "Ha! Whatd'ya think of that?," he yelled.

Katz didn't know what to think of it.

"God, what is it?," he said. "Who are they?" He picked up the album cover and flipped it over.

"It's the new thing, baby. I don't even know what to call it. They're from Frisco. It's crazy, ain't it?"

It was and it sure had a hell of a pulse. They waited till the last note faded out before they put down the headphones.

"That was amazing. Thanks, man. I gotta get that."

Johnny B tenderly took the record off the turntable and slid it into the jacket, revealing a book splayed face down on the desktop.

"What's this?" Katz asked. "'Message to the Blackman in America'? That doesn't sound too catchy."

"Ever hear of Elijah Muhammad?'

"Is he the guy with Ali?"

"Kind of the other way around. He's Supreme Minister of the Nation of Islam."

"You're into that?"

"Just reading it, trying to see what it's all about. Don't worry, my man, I won't kill you. Yet. So what's up? Why're you here?'

"I'm working on the Brenda Queen shooting."

"Okay, I get it. You saw old Johnny B's article and thought you'd see if there was a connection. That's some damned good police work, man. You're a regular Mannix!"

"I'm just feeling my way, really. So what's the story there?"

"It is a crying shame, man. You know who's on Stax/Volt, right?"

"Of course. Otis, Pickett, Sam and Dave, Brenda Queen."

"That's right, but did you know that Atlantic used to hold all the rights to their master tapes?"

"Used to."

133

"Right, before they just got bought by Warner Brothers. The contract they had with Stax said that if Atlantic ever got sold, the tapes would go to whoever bought them."

"Okay."

"Which means that all those tapes of Otis and Brenda Queen and everyone else belong to Warner Brothers now, not Atlantic, and not Stax/Volt."

"So she was going to be on Warners too."

"Right."

"So what does that have to do with her getting shot?"

"You're the cop, man. You tell me. There's more to the story though. Stax still has all the magic in the studio."

"Booker T and the MG's."

"Right, they're still the house band down there and Hayes and Porter are still the producers."

Katz tried thinking like a cop but he couldn't even find the right questions to ask, never mind the right answers. He tried to work the tapes angle.

"She was just getting started," he said, "so they probably didn't have nearly as many tapes of her as they did of the other guys."

"That's true and that may be why Stax thought they had a shot at keeping her. They were supposed to send somebody up to talk to her about it, I heard. Guess that's not going to happen now."

This was going nowhere. Katz couldn't help himself. He started thinking like a lawyer. Who would have something to gain – or lose – if she left Stax for Warners?

"Just to confuse things further," Johnny went on, "Warners is going to be putting together all the tours now, not Stax. That means a whole lot of new fingers in the pie."

"And a whole lot of old fingers out."

"Man, don't try writing for a living. That is a horrible metaphor. I'm ashamed we went to the same school, honestly."

"You know what I mean. Whoever was doing the tours for her was going to get screwed."

"That's right. Now that's something I can find out for you pretty quick."

"No need," Katz said. "I know who that is."

23

All Katz knew about 16th St. was it was the quickest way to get from GW to Hofberg's Deli. He was always so fixated on the Four Jacks jammed full of pastrami waiting for him there that he never even glanced at the houses but, now, even in the fading twilight, he could see why they called it the Gold Coast. The homes, so stately and beautiful, were amazing enough, but that Negroes owned almost every one of them absolutely floored him.

He made his way over to 18th and made a right where it dead ended with Colorado, right at Rock Creek Park. He fished his briefcase out of the cruiser and took in the house. The stone arches over the front porch must have set him back plenty. A big corner lot, a double chimney, and the Park at your front door? Walker Thomas must have done all right by Brenda Queen.

Katz hadn't called ahead because he wanted to see Thomas' face when he told him his name. He rang the doorbell. In a few seconds, a dapper man with a process, maybe in his late thirties, opened the door.

"Mr. Thomas?"

Thomas gave him the once over but showed no surprise that a cop was at his door.

"I'm Patrolman Katz, MPD."

His expression didn't change. Was he a hell of an actor or did someone else call Lisa?

"Okay. Is this about Brenda or something else?"

"Brenda. I looked through the file to see if anyone had talked to you yet. It didn't look like it so I thought I'd come by just to ask you about that night, if you don't mind."

"I'm expecting someone in a few minutes. How long's this going to take?"

"That really depends on you, I guess."

Thomas checked his watch.

"All right. Let's get it over with. Come on in."

He led Katz from the foyer into a wide open living room with a wall of windows facing the park. African masks framed a green and red striped dashiki hanging on the wall over a dark gray leather sofa that filled the wall across from the windows. A drop cloth covered whatever sat at the wall to their right.

"Forgive the mess. I'm having some work done. "

He gestured Katz to the other side of the room then extended his arm to the wall above the drop cloth.

"What do you think?"

It looked like it was going to be some sort of mural. He could make out the pencil outlines of a black face in profile and a warrior standing spear in hand. A rainbow arced behind them from one side of the wall to the other.

"Wow," seemed the best response. "Are you painting that?"

"No, no. I've got a decorator. Very talented guy named Rodney Davis. He's the one I'm waiting on, actually. Let's talk back here."

He led him down a hallway to a dining room dominated by a long dark wood table, probably mahogany, Katz guessed. He took a seat and pulled a pad and pencil from his briefcase. Thomas sat across from him.

"Am I right that no one from MPD's talked to you?"

"You are."

"I understand you were at the Howard the night Miss Queen was shot."

"Who told you that?"

"Does it matter?"

"No, I'm just curious why that would even come up. But, yeah, I was there and it was horrible. Seeing your wife shot dead, out of nowhere. Horrible."

137

"Tell me what you saw."

Thomas took a deep breath. His eyes looked weaker.

"When the show started, I was back in Emmett's office, Emmett Crowe, the GM, counting the take. When we were through, I went out to sit in the back row like I usually do -- did -- to catch her set. I had no idea what had happened to Dr. King or what was going on outside until this bunch of kids burst in from the back and started carrying on about him being shot and raising all kinds of hell. I jumped up and parked myself in the aisle to keep them from coming down to the stage and then I hear a couple shots – pow! pow! – off to my left --"

"Which way were you facing then?"

"Towards the back. And then I hear another couple shots from the right and the left. Now everybody's running back *out* of the place. I turn back to the stage and I see Jerome and Edward and James but I don't see Brenda, so I fight my way down the aisle --"

"Which one?"

"The middle one, and I get down front, and then I see her, laying on her back. I ran up the side closest to her and that's when I saw the blood. She was already gone. I never had a chance to say goodbye, tell her I loved her, nothing."

He popped up from his seat and disappeared into the next room. He came back in a few seconds with a tissue in his hands. His eyes brimmed with tears.

"It was rough, man. Still is."

Katz nodded and waited for him to pull himself together. When he sat back down, Katz asked "Do you know whether anyone had a reason to kill her?"

Thomas folded his arms and thought a moment before answering.

"You know, I'll be honest with you. My mind has wandered that way a few times, but I can't bring myself to

138

think that way. I have to believe it was just an accident, just her time."

Katz took his time writing his notes before asking the next question.

"You were her manager too, weren't you?"

"Yes, I was. Always made sure she was treated fair and square. Lots of vultures out there."

"Sure. Like Warner Brothers?"

Thomas seemed to stiffen.

"She was on Stax."

"I know, but I thought I read she was going to go to Warners because of some squabble between Stax and Atlantic."

"That was something I was trying to work out for her, make sure she was protected."

And you too, Katz thought, but he said "Did you know Albert Reynolds?"

"Of course."

"And you know that he's dead too?"

"Yes."

Katz waited for more. Thomas cocked his head at him, then pushed his chair back from the table.

"Wait a minute now, sonny. Where're you going with all this?"

"Nowhere. I'm just asking questions."

Thomas jumped up, knocking his chair back into the wall.

"You think I had something to do with this, don't you? Well, you're full of shit! That woman was my wife, my life! Why in the hell would I want to kill her?"

"I'm just a cop investigating a case, Mr. Thomas. I'm not --"

A voice called out from the living room.

"Walker? Where are you?"

Thomas fumbled his way past Katz. Katz followed him back into the living room. A tall thin black man in a black turtleneck and black leather bell bottom pants entered from the other side.

"Oh, you have company! Serious company! Aren't you going to introduce us?"

Thomas gritted his teeth.

"This is Officer Katz. He was just leaving."

The black man extended his hand.

"I'm Rodney, Walker's --"

"Decorator," Thomas said. "My appointment, officer? You can show yourself out."

Now Rodney's eyes welled up. He glared at Thomas, then strode past him to the back of the house. Thomas watched him disappear, then turned back to Katz, his eyes full of fire.

"There's the door," he said. "Don't come back without a warrant."

Katz watched him turn to follow Rodney, then let himself out and got in the cruiser. He had just made the turn back onto 18th St. when a glare of light from behind Thomas' house caught his eye. Between the bushes, he saw Thomas embrace his decorator.

24

"Whooee! Bubba!," Tiny yelled. "Look who's back!"

Bubba squinted through the windshield back up the alley that was Wiltberger Street. He shielded his eyes, then broke into a wide smile.

"Our boy Leroy!"

He tooted the horn a few times. Leroy threw up a hand. Bubba climbed out of the cab. Tiny came to his side to wait for him.

"Hustle on up now," he called out, "it be dark 'fore you get here."

Leroy didn't crack a smile, just kept coming at his own pace.

"What's that smell, Tiny?" Bubba said, loud enough for Leroy to hear. "Smell like shit, don't it?"

"Smell worse 'n shit. Smell like po' people shit! Worse kinda shit!"

Leroy shook his head.

"Funny though," Bubba said. "I thought them down there'd been resurrected. They shit should smell better, huh?"

"Should. But don't. Hoo, that some bad shit!"

As Leroy drew closer, they backed away, waving their hands underneath their noses. When he finally got to them, he reached out to give Bubba a soul shake but Bubba threw his hands behind his back.

"No, bro', oh no. You too funky to touch. Whyn't you go back down there, huh?"

"Union got 'em to rotate us out. Your turn's comin', bro, just you wait."

Around the middle of May, about 800 marchers arrived in Washington to carry out one of Martin Luther

King's last crusades, a poor people's campaign aimed at getting Congress to pass an economic bill of rights that would lift people of all races and nationalities out of poverty. The government let them camp out on a strip of the Mall along the Reflecting Pool that the organizers deemed Resurrection City. The permit required regular garbage disposal so Leroy and another hundred or so DC Sanitation workers drew duty that grew from nasty to gruesome as the City swelled to 3,000 and more. Now he was back on Wiltberger, helping Bubba and Tiny finish getting rid of the garbage that had piled up there since the riots.

He pointed to the square gray dumpster sitting behind the Howard.

"Finally got back to it, huh?"

The piles of paper bags, cardboard boxes, and loose garbage that filled the alley before the Department allowed its men back on the streets now just lined the walls.

Bubba pointed at a rat scurrying between Tiny's legs.

"Even yo' girlfriend happy to see you back, man," he said. Tiny's massive belly quivered as he giggled.

"Least I don't eat no rat pussy," Leroy said.

"No one talkin' 'bout yo' mama now," Bubba said.

"Don't start on my mama, Bubba."

"I'm sorry, man. That was a mistake. I apologize. It's yo' grandma you livin' with, right?"

"Yow!" Tiny yelled and clapped his hands.

Leroy stalked back to the dumpster and threw the lid open.

"Stand back, motherfuck. Here come the resta your kin."

Rats poured out in every direction.

"Go on now, babies,? Leroy yelled to them. "Go find yo' poppa! That's right, There he is. 'Hi, poppa'. Say 'hi poppa'."

142

They watched the surging horde stream up and down the alley, under the truck, between and around them. They had seen the show before. In thirty seconds, it was over. Leroy pulled a do-rag out of his back pocket, tied it over his nose and mouth, and walked back to the dumpster, flipping the lid back down.

Bubba hopped in the cab and started up the truck. He pulled forward, then angled back until Leroy held up a hand. He and Tiny rocked the dumpster into position. When Leroy pointed to Bubba, he pulled the stick that sent steel arms into the slots on either side of the box. He lifted it and tilted it forward until the lid dropped open and it vomited months' worth of wet, foul, rancid crap into the belly of the truck. Bubba reversed the sticks to smack it back down on the pavement.

Leroy leaned over to look in. There was still three feet of shit stuck in there.

"Bounce it!" he yelled up to Bubba.

Bubba lifted and lowered it hard a few times, then tipped it back up over the truck. Some more bags and loose junk slid in but Leroy knew there was more. He prepared for the worst.

When the box came down again, he peered back in to see a solid wall of bags and cans and glass wedged together at the bottom. He pointed at Tiny who helped him pirouette the box at an angle to the truck. Then they slammed it to the ground and watched what they hoped was everything left slide into the alley. Tiny watched Leroy poke his head in.

"Shit's still in there, man," Leroy said.

Tiny reached in and pulled the lip of a bag towards him, then cradled it in his arms and walked it to the truck. Leroy followed suit, then Bubba, until they got to the bottom. Leroy lifted the last bag out and watched it fall apart in his hands, all kinds of crap coating his legs and his shoes.

"Jesus motherfuckin' goddamn shit!" he screamed and kicked his feet loose from the pile below him. Something hard went spinning under the truck. Bubba and Tiny bent down to collect the mess while he got down on his knees and looked under the truck. When he saw what was there, he reached back for a plastic hot dog package and used that to pick it up.

"Yo," he said.

Bubba and Tiny looked at him, then down at the gun in his hand.

"Oh fuck," Tiny said.

"What you gonna do with that?" Bubba said.

Leroy tried to spin the cylinder but it was stuck. He tried to finger out the goop in one of the chambers but couldn't clear it out. He pointed it up the alley and squinted through the sight, then held it in place as he spun slowly to face Bubba.

"Hey, Bubba?" he said.

"Yeah?" Bubba said.

"What was that about my grandmomma?"

25

The day that Lisa left, two weeks and four days ago, Katz fell into a routine that was little more than plant life. On patrol from eight in the morning till four in the afternoon Sunday through Tuesday, off on Wednesday, then on from four to midnight Thursday through Saturday. No matter when they went out, everything was quieter than it was before the riots. Fewer stores open meant fewer people on the streets. Fewer bars open meant fewer drunks, fewer fights, fewer robberies. The riot blocks were all empty all the time. Crumbles of brick and glass lay just where they fell, strewn below the charred frames that stood invisible to everyone but the cops and bums who still had a reason to be there. Even on the blocks that bore no visible scar, there still seemed to be something that just felt different, something hard to define, less a tension or a fear than a wariness, a dull numbing throb like a shock wave that still pushed between not just whites and Negroes, but everyone, driving them all further and further apart.

Katz hated that throb but he savored the lull. He needed the relief, from his marriage, the riots, the daily grip of the job. Outside of a woman stabbed to death in a condemned building where the new freeway was going in next to HQ, nothing was going on in the First. When they needed some action, they rolled to whatever the radio squawked about almost anywhere. They broke up a fight over three dollars at Benny's Rebel Room on 14th. They backed up an abortion raid at a doctor's office on I Street. They spent an hour and a half prying open the trunk of a '63 Falcon where two guys dumped a woman after holding her up outside a liquor store on South Dakota Avenue Northeast.

When Katz got home, he called in dinner from Pot O'Gold or Eddie Leonard's, watched the local news on 9 so he could catch Warner Wolf's shtick, then Cronkite, then turned the dials to see if there was anything worth watching afterwards. When there wasn't, like tonight, he'd put the Senators on the radio and listen with one ear while he noodled around on the guitar, did the Post crossword puzzle, then noodled around some more, wrapping the evening up with an aimless walk up to Dupont Circle or through Georgetown, thinking only about how he could get Lisa to come back without changing his plans in the slightest. He'd finish wandering a little after 10 and be in bed by 11, sometimes managing to make it through Carson's monologue but most times not.

Their first night apart, he called Lisa's mother's house to try to talk to her.

"Hi, Sheila! This is Jake! How are you?"

Silent for a good long time, then more angry than he ever heard her before.

"How am I? How do you think I am, Jake?"

"I know. I'm sorry this is happening. For all of us."

"'For all of us?' Oh, please, Jake, am I supposed to feel sorry for you? For what? Putting my daughter's life in jeopardy? Scaring her – and me – to death? While you play your little cops and robbers games? What's happened to you? What's going on in your head?"

"That's what I want to talk to Lisa about. Is she there?"

"Oh!" An ear-splitting crack speared Katz's ear. He could see the phone bouncing off the kitchen wall. He laughed every time he saw her pull that trick in person, usually when one of her sons was giving her some long distance *tsuris*. It wasn't quite as funny being on the other end.

He rehearsed his lines.

"Lisa, this is Jake. I love you," which was true.

146

"Lisa, this is Jake, I'm sorry," which was also true, but given her mother's reaction, probably needed more work.

"Lisa, this is Jake. Please, honey, come back. It's safe now, I promise," which was just a lie.

Sheila was back on the line.

"Have you found the guy who called her?"

"Is that you asking or her?"

"Would the answer be different?"

"Can I please talk to her?"

"Have you found him?"

"No."

"Have you quit?"

"No."

"Then she doesn't want to talk to you."

"Tell her I sent the check."

"What check?"

"To GW. She'll know. I sent it today."

"I'll let her know."

"Sheila, Mrs. Rubin, please, just put her on."

"Jake, you listen to me. I love you like a son but Lisa is my daughter. I will not let you hurt her or put her in harm's way. You made a vow to each other, Jake --"

He heard yelling in the background, then Sheila's muffled yelling, then two people's muffled yelling, then Sheila very clearly yelling "Fine! Fine!"

"Jake," she told him, "I've said all I'm going to say. You know what you have to do."

"Sheila --"

"Goodbye, Jake."

He waited for Mike Epstein to bat in the sixth before he went out. Epstein was his favorite Nat, not because he was such a great player, but because he was a Jew too. When Katz heard him launch a two-run homer to put the Senators ahead 4-2, he put on his headphones and dialed the game up on his transistor. He headed down the steps to the street, around the bend onto K, then up 25th to Penn, and hung a left toward Georgetown. From there, he got so caught up in the game, he lost track of where he was.

It was a matchup of the best starters on each club, Joe Coleman for Washington, Catfish Hunter for Oakland. Katz let out a little whoop when Coleman got Floyd Robinson to ground out to open the ninth and did it again when Jim Pagliaroni flew out to Del Unser in center. One out to go. Reggie Jackson at the plate. John MacLean, the color guy, said "With no one on, Joe should go right after him." Dan Daniel, the play-by-play man, agreed and so did Katz but, of course, the Nats being the Nats, Coleman walked him.

"Not what Joe wanted," Daniel said.

"Dipshit," Katz muttered.

When Rick Monday singled Jackson to second, Daniel said "And that will bring the go-ahead run to the plate in the form of Mike Hershberger."

"Fucking dipshit," Katz muttered.

"Here comes Manager Jim Lemon to the mound," Daniel said. "That could be it for Coleman. Darold Knowles has been warming in the pen so he should be ready."

"Not Darold Knowles!" Katz cried out loud, drawing a laugh from a guy passing by and a curious look from his girlfriend. He made a right off of M onto one of the less populated numbered streets. He'd seen Knowles give up big hits too many times when he pitched for the Phils.

"Stay with Coleman," he begged Lemon, this time to himself.

"Hershberger's only hitting .175," Daniel said, "but when he gets good wood on the ball, he can drive it a long way."

"He's a righty," MacLean said, "so it might make sense to leave the righty Coleman in rather than call for the lefty."

"No shit, Sherlock" Katz thought. He breathed a sigh of relief when he heard Daniels say "Jim's going to leave it up to Coleman," and clapped his hands in the air when he heard him call a high fly ball to right and the catch by Ed Stroud to wrap it up. Only then did he notice was heading down 34th St., just a block from Key Bridge but about a dozen blocks from home. He dragged himself back down M and got in bed to watch the 11 o'clock news on 9.

The headline story was the California primary. The polls had closed and the results were starting to come in. Bobby Kennedy was slightly ahead of Gene McCarthy. Julian Barber reminded everybody that Humphrey was still way ahead in the delegate lead even without campaigning anywhere.

Lisa loved Kennedy, more for his looks and his family's sad story than his politics, he always thought, but never said. He was Clean for Gene himself, mostly because the war was the only issue that mattered to him. Being a cop kept his deferment and so would law school but he didn't need a personal motive to hate what the war was doing to his friends, his country, his image of his country, and he wanted it to stop. Nixon kept promising he had a plan to end the war but never said what it was. Even if he spelled it out every detail, Katz wouldn't have believed him anyhow. He remembered what his eighth grade teacher told his class when he ran in '60: I wouldn't buy a used car from him, but I'd sure want him selling mine. Exactly right.

He fell asleep with the TV on and it woke him up sometime in the middle of the night. He rolled over to see Kennedy waving at a podium. He must have won. He rolled back over and heard him congratulate Don Drysdale, the

Dodger, for pitching his sixth straight shutout. He thanked his dog, his wife, and Rosey Grier, the football player. He said how much he wanted to end all the divisiveness in the country, between black and white, rich and poor, old and young, on the war and so many other things. Good luck on that, he thought, and pulled his bottom pillow up over his head.

He must have fallen back asleep because a loud babble woke him up. The announcer was talking about Kennedy being shot but why bring that up now? He flipped the pillow off. He saw distraught people in a ballroom, heard shouts and wails, and felt ice burst from his chest and down his arms and legs. His brain caught up to what his body was telling him a split-second later. He jumped to his feet and grabbed his head with both hands. Not possible, he thought, not possible, over and over. He looked at the clock. 3:15.

Lisa. She'll wake up to this. He had to be with her. It was three hours to Cherry Hill. If he left now, he could be there before she got up and still get back before his shift started at four. He hit the head, threw on what he wore last night, and ran to the car.

He kept the radio on WAVA to catch the latest details. Kennedy wasn't dead but his condition was critical. They had the guy who shot him but the police hadn't identified him. No one knew if he acted alone. Katz prayed it was just a terrible nightmare. He lost the station in the Harbor Tunnel and had to keep twirling the dial to find anything new. Some station was playing nothing but patriotic music. The Star Spangled Banner. Marches. God Bless America. Did he still?

The sun rose to meet him as he crested the Delaware Memorial Bridge. He was under a quarter tank but wouldn't stop. He got off the Turnpike at Exit 4. He'd be there in ten minutes. He looked at the dashboard clock. 6:17.

150

He pulled onto Cherry Hill Boulevard and rolled to a stop in front of his mother-in-law's house. It was what they called a Colonial, probably twice as big as the house he grew up in. Mrs. Rubin lived there by herself, now that Lisa and her brothers Neil and Jerry were gone. Mr. Rubin died in a car accident when Lisa was little. She told him his life insurance covered the mortgage so her mother could stay there without ever having to work.

The house was dark. The newspaper sat in the rack below the mailbox. He knew he ought to wait for some sign of life, but sitting there in the still light of dawn, knowing what lay in store for them, he had to keep fighting back the urge to knock on the door, break the news as gently as he could, buffet them from the storm that was sure to follow.

A milk truck pulled up behind him. The driver got out, popped a side door, and pulled out a half-gallon bottle. He circled around the back of the truck, up the driveway, and down the walk to drop it into the gray box by the door. They stopped delivering milk in Levittown right after the Acme came in and started selling it a lot cheaper. Katz wondered how long this luxury of life would go on in Cherry Hill.

The driver bent down to look at him through the passenger window. Katz threw him a salute. The guy paused for a second, then climbed back in the truck and pulled up to the next house at the bend ahead. When Katz looked back to Lisa's house, he saw Mrs. Rubin in her robe, reaching for the paper.

"Jake?" was all she got out before he got to her.

"Sheila! I need to tell you something."

"What? Why are you here? What time is it?"

"I have some bad news."

She looked at him, not comprehending anything. He held her by the shoulders.

"Bobby Kennedy was shot last night."

"What?"

"I didn't want Lisa – or you – to wake up to that alone."

She searched his face, trying to make sense of what he was telling her. She pulled the paper open. The headline said "Kennedy Takes Early Lead in California".

"The paper – "

"It just happened, around three o'clock this morning. I jumped in the car as soon as I heard. I had to be here, with Lisa."

Her shriek shattered the stillness. She howled her grief to the sky, then collapsed against him. He fell back, holding her to him as tightly as he could. She buried her face in his shoulder, her screams muffled but unrelenting. He rocked her back and forth. He heard footsteps run down the stairs inside. Lisa stared at them through the screen door. The same face, the same look he just saw on her mother.

"Jake? What's going on?"

"I didn't want you to hear the news without me."

"What news?"

Mrs. Rubin pushed herself off of Katz and turned to her daughter, tears rolling down her cheeks. Lisa turned to her.

"What?" she screamed. "What is it?"

"Bobby Kennedy," her mother said but couldn't go any further.

Lisa turned to Katz, her eyes already knowing what he was going to say.

"He was shot, last night. But he's still alive."

She clutched at the hair falling over her face and tried to yank it from her head, then ran screaming back up the stairs. Jake threw the door open and ran after her. He followed her into her bedroom. She turned on the small black and white TV that sat on her dresser and saw Roger

152

Mudd interviewing Senator Kennedy. She turned to him in disbelief.

"It's on film, Lisa. Believe me. He's –"

She threw up her hand to make him stop, stop time, stop the horror overwhelming her. Her mother came through the door and went to her side, stroking the back of her head. Katz watched them watch the local newsman confirm the horrible truth. He watched them embrace each other, bawling and sobbing. He circled behind them and rubbed Lisa's back. She stiffened and twisted away from his touch.

"Lisa --"

She turned to him, her hair pasted to her face with tears, eyes red with rage, and screamed.

"Go away! I don't want you here! I don't want to see you! Ever!"

Her mother pulled her closer.

"I was just trying, hoping, to make it easier --"

She screamed at him, eyes glaring.

"Does it look like you've made it easier? Does it?"

"Lisa, don't," her mother said. Lisa spun back to her and pushed her away.

"Don't, mother! Don't!"

She ran out of the room back down the hall. They heard a door slam. Katz wanted to follow her but Sheila blocked his way.

"Jake, don't, please. You know how she gets."

He did but this was the first time he ever heard her mother say she knew too.

"Why, Sheila? What sets her off like that?"

Sheila sighed, then motioned him to follow her back down the stairs. She led him through the dining room and out the back door to the patio. She turned to face him, her arms crossed tightly in front of her, literally holding herself together, he thought.

153

"You know Irv, her dad, died when she was very young."

"Mine did too," Katz said.

"Yes, I know that, but she was just six, Jake, a lot younger than you. And she saw it happen. Did she tell you that?"

Katz was amazed to hear he wasn't the only one holding things back.

"No. She just told me how he died and how much she missed him."

"What did she tell you?"

"He got hit by a car right after a football game."

"That's what happened, but it's not the whole story."

"What is the whole story?"

She stepped quietly down the patio to look up at a window. The curtain was closed. She stepped back to Katz.

"He took her to a high school football game, her first one. God, was she excited to go." She did nothing to stop the tears from sliding down her cheeks again.

"Her brother, Neil, the older one, was maybe a sophomore or junior then and he had made the team for the first time, so it was a big deal for the whole family. Plus, it was one of those big rivalry games, Cherry Hill West and Camden, so everybody there was excited. And, on top of all that, all the Cherry Hill people were white and the Camden people, a lot were colored, so you get the picture."

Katz got it.

"So Irv wasn't a big football fan. He didn't know a first down from a home run but he wanted his little girl to see her big brother play so they go, and they wind up sitting in a section where it's all Camden fans and all *schwarz*, except for him and Lisa, okay? So, the game goes on and Camden is beating us bad and there's nothing for them to cheer for until the very end of the game we finally score a touchdown or whatever. Lisa said they both jumped up and started cheering, and the Camden people started shouting at them. 'Sit down,' 'shut up', worse, I'm sure but this goes on till the end of the game until Irv gets them both out of there and into the parking lot. He doesn't remember where he parked, he's looking around a while, and then –"

She dug her tongue deep into her cheek and shook her head, then smacked her hands together, startling Katz.

"Bam! He gets hit by a car, right in front of her, dead before he hit the ground. The car takes off and she sees a black hand sticking out the window giving her the middle finger. She didn't even know what it was, but that's what she tells the police. Can you imagine? Can you picture that? Can you maybe understand a little better now?"

Lisa's resemblance to her mother was never more unmistakable than at this instant, the same sorrow etched into every pore.

"I'm so sorry, Mrs. Rubin," he said. "I had no idea."

She drew a deep breath.

"So, now you know. All her life, ever since, Neil, Jerry, and I have protected her, sheltered her, coddled her, however you want to say it. Maybe it's been too much, but if it was your child, you'd do the same thing, I guarantee you."

"I don't know what to say," Katz said.

"You never tell her I told you, okay? I'd never hear the end of it."

"No, I won't, I promise."

She reached out and gave him a hug. They held each other tightly.

"So now," she said, "You leave her alone for a while. Go back to Washington and take care of what you need to take care of, then maybe this will all work out. Maybe. I hope. I just don't know."

He squeezed her hand then walked back to his car. The seat was still warm.

He squinted into the sun and wondered how he and Lisa would ever stay together if they couldn't share anything that really mattered. Rather than a blessing, understanding his wife seemed like just another curse on such a cursed day in such a cursed country.

26

The last time he was home was the weekend before the riots, to say Kaddish on the tenth anniversary of the day his father disappeared. The curtains were open so he knew she knew by now. He pulled into the driveway and parked next to her car. He knocked on the door, then went back down the walk so she could see him through the window. He waved and mouthed "Hi, mom." She practically skipped to the door.

"Jake! *Tattelah*! What are you doing here?"

"I just wanted to be with you this morning."

She pulled him inside the house and hugged him.

"Oy, what a horror. First his brother, now him," she said.

It came from deep within him, first a shudder, then the sobs. She wrapped him in her arms.

"Jakey, Jakey. I had no idea he meant that much to you."

He clung to her, bawling out everything inside of him.

27

Scheingold was so excited he didn't wait for Katz to say hello.

"You know that contest they're running on WOL?"

Katz couldn't bring himself to tell him he didn't.

"Yeah?"

"I got a free ticket for you, if Lisa'll let you out."

Another thing he couldn't tell him.

"How'd you get it?"

"They did the same dopey thing they always do. They run the ad ten minutes after every hour so I dialed every number except the last one and waited for it. Boom, first one in!"

"And you missed the question."

"Of course. Who wants to win a raffle for a Caddy when the consolation prize is two tickets to see Smokey, the Mad Lads, Brenda and the Tabulations, the Artistics, I can't even remember them all."

"That's all one show?"

"Yep. Saturday night. DC Coliseum."

He hadn't been to a show since the riots. Maybe it wouldn't be safe. On the other hand, it could be just what he needed to get out of his funk. That was some show.

"Sounds great," he said. "I'll pick you up."

If it weren't for the marquee, it would be impossible to distinguish the Coliseum from the warehouses surrounding 3rd and M Northeast. It used to be an ice plant before it became a sports arena and still looked it.

It was also, for some unknown reason, the first place the Beatles ever played in the U.S, February 11, 1964, second semester freshman year. Weiss knew someone who knew someone and got tickets for him, Schein, and Katz. Weiss and Schein flipped out about it, but not Katz.

"Thanks, but no thanks," he told Weiss.

"What?" Weiss said. "You don't want to see the Beatles?"

Katz did want to see them but he was proud of his allegiance to soul music. He couldn't let himself go ape over a white group after he'd spent years badmouthing every one he heard on the radio so he told Weiss to find someone else to take his ticket. Weiss just shook his head.

"Too cool for the Beatles," he said. "Aren't you something?"

He had never been too cool for anything so he took pride in that too.

When they got back, Schein told him he never heard a note. "The only thing you missed was five thousand girls screaming their way through puberty."

It was only when the Beatles Second Album came out that April that he felt he missed something. Their covers of R&B classics like Roll Over Beethoven, You Really Got A Hold on Me, Money, Long Tall Sally, and Please Mr. Postman were as good as the originals, maybe better. He bought every album after that, pride intact.

Rows of wooden folding chairs filled the floor for tonight's show. An usher pointed them to their row about halfway to the stage at the far end. A comedian named Flip Wilson was doing his best to get the crowd's attention but no one was listening. In the glare of the lights, they were all there to see and be seen and the only other white face Katz saw was Scheingold's. He knew they'd be the center of everyone else's attention for a passing moment, but it wasn't the first time. There had never been a problem. Why would there be now?

Maybe because Crawford was striding up the aisle, with Wallace right behind him. His first impulse was to keep Scheingold out of whatever was about to happen.

159

"Schein, stop, go back," he called over his shoulder but Scheingold was pushing him forward. When he turned to look, he saw a crowd of brothers bumping Scheingold from all sides. They weren't there a minute ago. Then he got pushed back into Scheingold. A knot of guys, all young and black, were bumping them both.

"Whoa," Katz said, "there's room for everybody." The dude at his shoulder glared at him over the top of his shades.

"Hey!" Scheingold yelled. "My wallet! Where's my wallet?"

Katz turned to see his friend, red, shaking, and pointing a finger at a thin guy in a porkpie hat. The guy spread open his hands.

"What wallet, man? The fuck you talkin' about?"

Katz reached back for his own wallet but felt another hand there first. He grabbed it and spun around to face the dude in the shades.

"Keep your fuckin' hands to yourself, pal!"

"Give me back my wallet!" he heard Scheingold squeal. Katz tried to turn back but he could barely keep his balance as the dude and his buddies elbowed and shouldered him away.

"You want your wallet?" the guy in the porkpie hat said. "Come get your wallet."

He balled his left hand into a fist and beckoned Schein to him with the other. Katz flailed to get to them.

"I'm a cop!" Katz yelled. "Leave him --"

He heard a sharp crack and saw wood shower over him. The world slowed to a crawl. The ground rose to meet him and smacked his face. Pain grabbed his head and squeezed hard. He rolled to his back. He opened his eyes to see a folding chair rise, then fly at his head. He heard his head crack, then watched blood spurt over his eyes and down

160

his face. The noise was terrific. He couldn't open his left eye. He squinted with the other to see the guy in shades straddling him, holding the leg of a chair like a tomahawk.

"You want more, o-fay? Come on!"

Everything around him swirled. He rolled over on to his stomach and took a kick in the ribs, then one in the left cheek. All he could hear was cheers. He swatted at the feet in front of him and pushed himself to his knees. A hard kick in the ass sent him sprawling forward.

He crawled back on to his knees and looked up into the grinning face of the guy who started with Schein.

"Not so tough now, are we, my man?"

Katz took his measure from the floor then pushed off with both feet and tackled him low, just the way they taught him in high school. The guy went down hard on his back and the scrappy little Hebe pushed him down the floor until he felt hands grabbing at his back and his legs. He sprung forward to straddle the other man's waist and threw punch after punch into his face, his chest, whatever he left uncovered. Over the roar around him, he heard the comedian yell "Look at the fight, man! Look at the fight!"

He felt hands pulling at his shoulders but he couldn't stop, wouldn't stop until he punched himself out and let himself get tugged away. He closed his eyes and raised his arms to protect himself from the next onslaught. He felt the ground fall away as two giant arms reached around him from behind and lifted him off his feet and down a row of chairs. The blood surged through his temples, then drained back away as he twisted his head far enough to see Wallace's face straining from the load. Then he saw nothing.

28

Katz sensed he was flat on his back but somehow in motion. A hard bump jolted him enough to try to see where he was. His left eye squinted into the lights above him, but he couldn't open his right. He turned his head to the left to see Wallace on a chair, leaning back, hands in his lap. He groped to think why. He turned his head far enough the other way to make out a bottle swaying on a hook on a pole. He followed the tube hanging from the bottle down to his arm. He looked up into the smiling face of a Negro woman he didn't think he knew hovering over him.

"Well, hello! How do you feel?"

Like shit, he thought. His head throbbed, his face felt stiff, and his ribs were killing him.

"Where am I?" he asked.

"You're in an ambulance, heading for D.C. General. We should be there in about two minutes."

Katz shook his head like he understood but he didn't. He closed his eyes and tried to remember how he wound up in an ambulance. Wallace had something to do with it but all he could pull up was his face. At the Coliseum. A jumble of pain and shards of memories cascaded through his head. He opened his eyes and turned to him.

"You pulled me out of there."

Wallace shrugged. "They pay me to keep the peace, so that's what I did."

Another memory tugged at Katz.

"Schein. What happened to Scheingold?"

"He your fat friend?"

Katz nodded.

"Crawford pulled him out of there, got him back to the locker room with you. He waited for the ambulance. Then, I don't know."

Katz nodded again then heard Wallace say exactly what he was thinking.

"I hope he had the sense to get his fat ass out of there."

A sharp sting of pain sliced down from the top of his head. He reached up to feel the spot but the nurse gently grabbed his wrist.

"Best to leave that alone, honey. That's going to take a lot of stitches to close up."

Katz needed to rest his eyes. When he got the left one open again, he was blinded by a bank of bright lights overhead. He tried to lift a hand to block the glare but couldn't do it. He felt unconsciousness overtake him.

The next time he woke up, the light was streaming through a window. He felt a warm breeze cuddle his face and turned to see airy white curtains puff and lift. He watched them dance till his right eye filled with tears. Birds chirped. An ambulance siren rose then died. He squinted to see the back of a big black man pass by his doorway, a cloud of cigarette smoke trailing behind him. When he passed back and saw Katz looking at him, he came in and stubbed out his butt in the ashtray by the door.

"Detective Wallace?"

"Officer. How you feeling?"

The disjointed fragments of the night before came rocking back through Katz's memory. He tried to pull them together but the only thing that came through clearly was Wallace carrying him up and away from people who were trying to kill him. Tears welled now in both eyes. He pulled the sheet up to cover his face until he could get his act together. When he was close enough, he pulled it down to see Wallace standing at the window, eyes closed, basking in the warmth.

"I'm not trying to make detective," Katz said. "You need to know that."

Wallace didn't move.

"Never said you were," he said.

"Your buddy did, what's his name?"

Wallace pulled a chair over to the side of Katz's cot.

"Crawford? He's a hothead, liable to say pretty much anything." He sat down and leaned towards Katz. "So, how you feeling this morning?"

"What time is it?"

"About eleven. They finished up with you around ten last night so you had a pretty good night's sleep."

"What'd they do to me? Where's a mirror?"

"I don't know if I'd be runnin' to look in any mirrors for a while." He wiggled a finger at Katz' face. "You got some nasty bruises there, a busted lip they stitched up, a hell of a shiner, and a big hole they sewed up on top there. Also got a wrap around your ribs and I don't know what else. You gave the docs a good workout."

Katz now felt the pain and the stiffness everywhere Wallace pointed.

"When did you get here?"

"Been pacin' out there all night, man, just waitin' for you to come around."

"Really?"

"No, man, not really," he laughed. "I'm just havin' some fun with you. Got here maybe fifteen minutes ago. If you hadn't woke up by the time I finished my cigarette, I was going to wake you up. We need to talk."

"About what?"

"About our case."

Katz noted the 'our' but held his tongue.

"Why? What's up?"

164

"I got a call from Walker Thomas' lawyer. He wasn't too happy about you talking to his client without him being there. I wanted to tell him I didn't know anything about it either but figured I ought to talk to you before I said anything."

"Why did he have to be there? I was just asking him some questions. I didn't accuse him of anything."

"That's not the way Thomas took it. You know, I might've been able to help if you'd let me know you were gonna talk to him."

Katz spent a while thinking about how to answer. Yesterday, he would've told him he didn't want to waste his time arguing with him about it. Today, though, he wouldn't talk that way to the man who saved his life. Out of options, he decided the only way to answer was to actually, for once, say what was on his mind.

"I had another reason to talk to him, one that I didn't want you there for."

"What was that?"

"My wife got a threatening phone call from someone, someone she said sounded black."

"Okay. So?"

Wallace's confusion looked real enough so Katz went ahead.

"The guy basically threatened me – and her – saying I needed to back off. If I didn't, he said he knew where we lived."

Wallace still didn't seem to understand.

"So what, you thought it might have been Thomas?"

"Yeah."

"Okay."

"Or you."

This time, it took Wallace a while to answer.

"So you wanted to see how Thomas would react when you introduced yourself."

"Right."

"And if I was there, and I was the one who made the call, you thought it'd give me a clue you were lookin' for me, right? Give me a chance to cover my tracks or somethin'?"

"Right."

"Okay. So how did he react?"

"I don't think he made the call."

"Uh huh. So now, you were looking to see how I reacted too, right?"

"Right."

"And how'd I do?"

Katz had come this far saying what he really believed, so he said it again.

"I don't think you made the call either."

"I don't know about Thomas, but I can tell you you're right this time. I did not call your wife."

"I know you didn't."

"Then who's left?"

"Crawford?"

"I know that man and I can tell you that's not his style but, okay, let's leave him on the table for now. Who else?"

"The only other person I can think of is Jerome Terry."

"Who's he?"

"One of the Jacks that backed up Brenda Queen."

"Why would he make that call?"

"Because he and Brenda apparently had a long-time thing going on and he might've thought I knew about it."

"Did you know about it?"

Katz nodded. "Yeah. Edward – one of the other Jacks – told me about them."

"But Jerome was on stage with her when she died, right? You think he had a triggerman do it?"

"I don't think anything yet. I'm waiting to see where the evidence leads me."

Wallace snuck him a small smile.

"I like the way you think."

"I'm sorry I thought it might have been you."

"If I was in your shoes, I would've put me on that list too. Don't worry about it."

"I'm glad I'm wrong."

"So let's talk to this other Jack and see what he can tell us."

"And what about the lawyer? What are you going to tell him?"

"The truth, just what you told me. Won't be the first time I covered my partner's ass."

29

Lord, Cora Ann Mullins thought, it is hot. Am I crazy to be doing this in the middle of a June day? What if I miss that bus and have to wait out there a half hour for the next one, if it even shows up? She looked down the concrete staircase leading down to two and pictured the one below it. Down's bad enough but all the way back up after being out in that sun? She heard a door slam below and saw a couple of bushy heads flying up the steps from one. Too young or too old to be any of hers. Good thing for them too, she thought, running around like maniacs, cackling and hee-hawing. Animals. What was the world coming to? That steeled her spine to do what she started out to do.

She reached out for the railing, got a good firm grip on it, and pulled herself down to the first step, putting her left foot down, then her right one next to it. The little banshees thundered up from below and zigzagged past her, the last one pretending to lose his balance.

"Oh, no," he yelled, "I'm falling! Someone help meeee!"

"That's just what I'm talkin' about," she called after them, not hearing whatever they yelled back down at her. "No sense at all."

When she finally got to the ground floor, she shifted her straw bag from her left hand to the right and pushed through the door out into the sunshine. Hot as it was out here, it was still cooler than up there, what with all the windows shut so the bugs wouldn't get at them. It was bright too, but she tugged down the wide brim of her soft white hat with the little bunches of plastic grapes and cherries all around the top and peeked down Savannah Street in the direction of the bus stop three blocks away around the bend. She pushed up the sleeve of her jacket to take a look at her watch. 11:35. The bus came at noon -- supposed to come at noon, she reminded herself. Her luck, it'd be on time today.

She drew herself up and took a deep breath. She knew every step of this walk, took it every working day for thirty-two years till last September when she retired from the cafeteria at St. Elizabeth's. She didn't miss any of it, not the walk, not the bus, not the job, not the crazy people she doled the food out to or the crazy people she worked for. If she could, she'd never ride a bus again, but today, she told herself, she had to. If I had a car, she thought, I'd be there in two minutes. Keep the window down, let the wind blow right through me. But no. Six people living up in that two-bedroom hothouse, none of 'em got a car.

She pushed herself up the sidewalk, thinking wicked thoughts about every one of them. The one that got a baby ain't got no husband. The other one's got a husband except he ain't her husband, he someone else's, and the only one that got a job got no sense, no sense at all.

"Cora," she asked herself, "why God make you carry all these burdens? He really think you can handle this? Why? And why me?" She felt little streams of sweat snake their way down and over her ample cheeks into the folds of her neck. She could picture that bus stop. Better be room on that bench. Better make room. She praised God for not making her have to transfer. Bet they never transferred in Georgetown.

She saw it now, just a little over a block away. She pushed her sleeve back up. 11:50. She needed to sit down. Why was she doing this anyhow, trying to protect someone who didn't care enough to protect himself? Why am I suffering when he's the boneheaded child who should be payin' for his own stupidity? Why isn't his momma makin' this trip? Right, the mama with the other one's husband. She couldn't tell right from wrong if they both stood up and

169

introduced themselves to her. No, it was on her to show them the way, just like always. Lord, thank you for giving me the wisdom and the strength.

She staggered to the stop. The bench was empty and she dropped onto it with a loud grunt. She didn't have to push her sleeve up this time because it was glued with sweat right where she left it. 12:05. Why was she the only one there? Must have missed it. She prayed to God she hadn't and let out a whooping "Thank you, Jesus!" when the big white bus rolled up to the corner.

She paid her quarter and thumped into the seat behind the driver. She tugged the window open to let the wind blow through her but the traffic was so thick the bus barely moved, inching up 23rd Street, then all the way down Alabama and all the way up Nichols. She was hotter when she got off the bus than she was when she got on.

She looked down into her bag. The toilet paper she stuffed in there obscured the view but she reached down under it to make sure she hadn't accidentally dropped what she had come all this way to deliver. When she felt the barrel inside the saran wrap, she pulled her hand out like she'd touched fire.

What was that idiot grandchild of mine thinking when he brought this into my house? Waving it at everyone, at me! Blam, blam, blam, he goes, like a five-year-old! Let him look for it, wonder who took it. I'll tell him when I'm good and ready. Thinks that little of his grandma and that little baby. Ashamed to call him mine.

She crossed the street, paying no mind to the horns honking her to hurry up. She reached out for the railing and put her left foot on the first step up to the station house, then her right one right beside it.

30

The docs released Katz after two days but confined him to bed rest so he was denied even the small pleasures of plant life. He made it through one day and most of one night, then showed up at the station at six the next morning, declaring himself fit for work. They kept him on desk duty, letting him walk only far enough to sit in on Jarvie's next session.

Jarvie saluted him when he came through the door, then did a double take. He climbed the steps to take a look up close. He took in the eye, the lip, the stitches crossing his scalp, and winced.

"Wow. What happened to you?"

"Took a little bit of a beating."

"On the job?"

"No. Just a fun evening out."

Jarvie nodded, then cocked an eye at him.

"You and Wallace have an exchange of views?"

"Yeah, but this wasn't it. We're cool now."

"Good to hear. Well, sit down and take it easy. Don't let 'em push you back out on the street too fast."

"I won't. Thanks."

Jarvie went back down to the front and handed out the day's case.

"Welcome back, all. It's good to see so many recidivists. Today we're going to talk about a case the Supreme Court decided a few months ago. It's called Simmons v. U.S. Anybody familiar with it?"

Not a hand went up.

"Great, then I can bullshit you all I want. So here's what happened. A couple of guys, including one Mr. Thomas Earl Simmons, figured they'd warm up on a cold February afternoon in Chicago by ducking into a savings and loan and holding it up. It took them about five minutes to do the job. They were either confident enough or stupid enough to pull it off without masks, and to use a T-Bird as the getaway car. A teller told the Bureau about the car and within an hour they spotted it and discovered it belonged to Mr. Simmons' sister-in-law. Cut to the chase, she gives the agents some pictures of Mr. Simmons and they take them to the bank to show them to the five, count 'em, five employees who had a front row seat to the whole show. Every one of them i.d.'d Mr. Simmons as one of the robbers, and at trial, they all step up and do it again, so Mr. Simmons does not pass Go and proceeds directly to jail. That's pretty much the whole story. Anyone see any problems here?"

Katz wondered if they showed them photos of other guys too, but he kept it to himself. No one else said anything either.

"No? Well, Mr. Simmons' lawyer did. He reminded the Court that it had decided a couple of cases last year that said if the police used identification procedures that were constitutionally flawed, the conviction had to be thrown out. So, what do you think? Did these procedures deprive Mr. Simmons of his constitutional right to due process of law?"

Again, nothing from anyone.

"Okay, then let me try this on you. Do you think it would make a difference if they were only visible at the bank for, say, ten seconds rather than five minutes? What if they robbed the place at night, in the dark, rather than broad daylight? Would showing the tellers the pictures of just one guy in that situation be too unfair to stand up in court?"

"Yeah," Katz heard himself say, "I think it would."

"Ah, Officer Katz speaks up. Why do you think so?"

"Because there's a bigger chance the witnesses would get it wrong. They wouldn't have had the same chance to make a good ID. But seeing the guys in broad daylight,

172

without masks, for five minutes? I think it'd be okay to use the pictures."

"Really? But just his picture? Wouldn't that make it seem the agents had zeroed in on this guy? Wouldn't that be kind of intimidating to the witness, like the FBI was kind of nudging them to say 'that's the guy' even if they weren't sure?"

"Did they do or say anything like that?"

"From the decision, it doesn't look like it."

"Then I'd say it's kosher."

Jarvie stroked his chin. "Hmm. Anyone agree with Judge Katz? Disagree?"

Silence reigned again.

"Judge Katz, the Court agreed with you. In Justice Harlan's words, what the cops did here was not 'so impermissibly suggestive as to give rise to a very substantial likelihood of irreparable misidentification.' Or, as you put it so well: It was kosher."

Katz felt a little swell of pride but when it subsided, he wondered if it was his special curse to have a head for something he didn't have his heart in.

31

When Wallace said to meet him at the Hawk 'n' Dove to talk about what they ought to ask James, Katz thought it was the perfect place. If there was any place in the city where both of them would feel at home, that was it. True to its name, the bar seemed to welcome everyone – whites, Negroes, Democrats, Republicans, hippies, Marines, eighteen-year olds, eighty-year olds, queers, and straights. Everyone seemed to get mellow at the Hawk.

Maybe Bobby Lima was the reason. A mix of white and black himself, maybe five-eight, thin and elegant, Bobby played everyone's favorites at the piano at the back of the room. Right now, he was having fun with "Mack the Knife," flashing his pearly whites.

Katz sang along to himself while he searched the room for Wallace. Through the gray haze of smoke, he saw him singing along too at a small round table by the wall to the left. He never saw him so relaxed, leaning back in his chair, casual jacket open over a dark brown shirt, collar flying wide. Whether it was the place, the singer, or the tumbler of brown booze in his hand, Katz didn't care. It was good just to see him happy about something.

He waited for the song to end before threading his way over.

"Detective?" he said and reached out his hand. Wallace shook his glass at him.

"Shush, man, it's Tom here, or Wallace, anything you want, except Detective."

Katz took the seat next to him so he could watch Bobby too.

"Sorry. Tom, I'm Jake."

He held out his hand again. Wallace raised his glass, then called out to Bobby.

"Hey, Bobby! Hey, man! How 'bout a Hundred Pounds of Clay?"

Bobby nodded to him and tickled the opening notes. They sang along with the table of white kids to their left all the way to the end. Bobby put a power finish to it and the room clapped its approval.

"Love this guy, man," Wallace said. "Better than the original, every time."

The waitress came over to take Katz' order.

"How are you, sweetie? What'll it be?"

"Miller High Life?"

"You got it. Refill, Tom?"

Hawkins drained his glass and held it out to her.

"Don't mind if I do, Carla. Thanks."

Carla took it and sashayed her way back towards the bar.

"I take it you're a regular?" Katz asked.

"I come when I can."

"It's a great place. I used to come up here with my girlfriend from GW all the time."

"'Used to'? She not your girlfriend anymore?"

"No," Katz said. "She's my wife."

"Hah!," Wallace laughed. "That's a good one, man!"

"No, I didn't mean it like that. She's still my girlfriend, but we're married now."

"Whatever you say, my man."

"You married?"

Wallace reached into his inside pocket and pulled out a pack of Kools. He slid one out and tipped the pack to Katz who waved him off. Wallace threw the pack on the table and lit up. Katz thought he didn't hear him so he asked again.

"I heard you the first time, man," Wallace said. "I'm just not sure I want to start lettin' you into my personal life just yet." He pointed at Carla heading back their way. "We'll see after this one."

She laid the tray down on the table and handed them their drinks. Wallace pointed at Katz.

"My man here says he used to come here with his girlfriend but he don't anymore, now that she's his wife."

Katz started to protest but Carla's laugh cut him off. She patted him on the wrist.

"Don't, honey. He's just trying to get a rise out of you. I know his game."

Katz threw up his hands in surrender.

"Henry back on the job?" Wallace asked her.

"Oh, yeah, he just needed a few days to calm down. He's been fine since."

Wallace leaned over to Katz to explain.

"Henry Lange's the guy who owns this place. Night of the riots, he got up on the roof, started shootin' all around."

"At who?" Katz asked. "No one rioted up on the Hill."

"That's right," Carla answered, "and he'll tell you that's why. 'Cause he was up there givin' 'em hell."

"That's crazy," Katz said.

"No, that's Henry," Carla said. "'Course sittin' in here all day chuggin' down Jack and listenin' to the sirens and the TV and all probably didn't help either."

"A man protectin' his property," Wallace said. "I'll drink to that. Nothin' crazy about it."

He lifted his glass, clinked it against Katz', and took a long swallow. When he put it down, he bellowed out "Woody! My man!"

Katz looked up to see a short balding guy with glasses behind Carla, holding her shoulders. He knew who he was: Schein's bookie.

176

"I'll be back to look after you in a little bit," Carla said and let Woody by. He pulled a chair over from the next table and joined them.

"How you, Tom?"

They shook hands and Wallace started to introduce him to Katz.

"No, I know you," Katz said. "From the Red Lion, right? You take bets from my friend Scheingold."

Woody slapped his hand to his chest and shook his head, aghast, the look of denial on his face so convincing that Katz was ready to doubt what he knew was true, until Wallace laughed out loud.

"You good, Woody, you good, man," he said.

Woody gave him a soul shake, then turned to Katz.

"Is he the chubby guy, with the bad beard?"

Wallace laughed even harder, rasping and coughing.

"Oh, Lord, that your fat friend from the Coliseum? That boy is nothin' but trouble."

Katz watched Woody reach into his shirt pocket, count out ten ten-dollar bills, and lay the stack in front of Wallace. Wallace smiled at him.

"Pascual's a hell of a pitcher." Woody said.

"Better than Monbo any day of the week," Wallace said.

Bobby Lima launched into Richie Valens' "Donna". The whole place sang along and cheered him off the stage with a standing ovation. When they sat back down, Woody asked Wallace, "Anything else I can do for you?"

Wallace took five tens off the top of the stack and left the rest sit there.

"Put that on the Yanks tonight."

"You're betting against the Senators?" Katz asked. "You're not a fan?"

"I am a fan," Wallace said. "Of winnin'."

Woody slid the tens off the table and into his pocket, then threw Wallace a salute.

"See you at the Lion, kid," he said to Katz and disappeared into the crowd. Wallace saw the puzzled look on Katz' face.

"What's up with you?" he asked.

"I just never heard of anyone betting on baseball."

Wallace hacked out a sharp laugh.

"Right, the Great American Pastime. What's your fatso friend bet on?"

"Football, basketball. Never baseball."

"I bet them too. Don't matter to me what it is, man, I'm just lookin' for some action."

Wallace fanned out the bills, counted them, and tucked them into his suit pocket.

"So you a Senators fan, huh?" he asked Katz.

"I root for them 'cause I'm here but I grew up a Phillies fan."

"Oh yeah, you from Philly?"

"Yeah, just outside."

"Basketball fan too?"

"Yeah, I love the Sixers, Wilt. He's so great."

Wallace looked impressed. "So you see Earl Monroe play up there?"

"You mean with the Bullets?"

"No, man, in high school. He went to school up there."

"I didn't know that."

"Thought you said you was a basketball fan."

"I am, I just never heard of him till he got to the Bullets."

"Never heard of Black Jesus. That's unbelievable, man, truly."

Katz let the dig pass. He threw down a couple chugs of his Miller and watched Wallace tap another cigarette out.

"So did you see him in Philly?" he asked.

"Naw, I go up to Baltimore every now and then to see him. Saw him play here in DC though, a couple years ago against Howard."

"Where'd he play?"

"Winston-Salem State. Beat Howard by a point. He was the whole show." He shook his head, savoring the memory. "Never seen anything like it. Dipsy doodles, in and out, pass, shoot, the best guard I ever saw."

"Better than Cousy? Or Jerry West?"

Wallace swallowed a drag and shot Katz a look that needed no explanation. Katz decided to shut his mouth again and scanned the crowd, looking for anyone or anything to divert his attention. He looked at his watch. When was Bobby coming back on? When he glanced back at Wallace, he was surprised to see him staring at him.

"So you a college boy, right?" he said.

"Yeah," Katz said. "GW. I graduated in '67."

"GW, huh? They even have a basketball team?"

Katz had been to a few games. They were terrible, but what he thought about now, for the first time, was that all their players were white. Over four years, he didn't remember ever seeing any Negroes play ball for or against them.

"Yeah," he said. "But they're awful."

"And they gave up football too, didn't they? Or did it give up on them?" Wallace snorted a laugh and took another drink.

"Yeah, that's probably more like it."

Katz decided it was time to start talking about what they ought to ask James, then head back home, when Wallace surprised him again.

179

"Now, football," he said, "that's really my game."

"To bet?"

"No, man, to play."

"Really? Where'd you play?"

"Linebacker."

"No, I mean like where, high school, college?"

"High school I was a fullback. At Alcorn State, they made me a linebacker."

"Where's that?"

"Mississippi. About 90 miles from Jackson, practically in Louisiana."

"When did you play there?"

"Graduated in '58."

"Did you grow up down there?"

Wallace swirled his drink and drained it.

"Yeah. Greenville. Up in the Delta?"

"I heard of it. Home of the blues."

"That's right. Like I say, I played a little in high school but never made it all the way through --"

"Wait a minute," Katz said. "How did you play in college if you never graduated high school?"

"Slow down, man. I'm getting' ready to tell you."

Katz grabbed his Miller and drained it. When he put it down, Wallace went on.

"I dropped out when I was in the tenth grade, 1950. I wasn't too much on studyin' and thought I'd go sign up and fight in Korea. So I did, but they decided I ought to be a MP so that's what I did for three years -- pick up drunk white boys in Seoul and put 'em in the stockade. That was my Military Occupational Specialty."

He snorted out another laugh. Katz kept on shutting up.

"But I also got my GED over there, which is how come I got to go to Alcorn. Now you see?"

180

Katz nodded.

"So how'd you wind up here?"

"When I got out of there, I had a teacher's certificate but nowhere to teach. Then one day I got a postcard from Marcus Morris, one of my MP buddies in Korea stationed up here at Fort Meade. Said the DC police were lookin' for brothers and he was going to apply, and did I want to join him. Man, I knew nothin' about DC or the PD so I asked him what he knew. He said they were serious, mostly because they were havin' trouble finding white boys to go into the ghettos, but he had a friend who signed up told him some other stuff he said I needed to know."

"Like what?"

"Like until about '61, black cops weren't allowed to arrest white folks. You know that?"

"What? No! Are you serious?"

"Yes, I'm serious. Brother found a white man holdin' a smokin' gun standin' over a warm dead man, he had to take him to a phone box, call it in, and hold him till a white boy come and arrest him."

Katz was speechless. Wallace was just getting started.

"And how 'bout this? You ever see a white cop and a black cop in a patrol car? I'm not talkin' about those Mod Squad jokers in plainclothes, I'm talkin' about uniforms."

He didn't wait for Katz to answer.

"Who you ride with?"

"Floyd Krebs."

"White boy?"

"Very white boy."

"That's the way it is, man. Marcus said they didn't even let blacks ride patrol at all, even together, till a few years back. They'd put the car down, take it out of service, before they'd let two brothers ride in one. All we could do is walk. Is that some shit or what?"

"But you still came up?" Katz asked. "Why?"

"Why? I had fifty-six hundred good reasons. That's what they were payin'. No way I'd make that as a teacher or anything else down there so I put my faith in Jesus and Marcus and pretty much took the next bus up."

Katz remembered Jarvie telling him there was more to the story. He'd probably never get a better chance to hear it than now.

"So how did you make Detective?" he asked.

The question drowned in the crowd's whoops for Bobby coming back to the piano. When the cheers died down, he repeated it. Wallace fixed Katz with a long stare. The crowd roared again as Bobby launched into the Del-Vikings' "Come and Go With Me." Wallace signaled to Carla for the check.

"Let's take a walk," he said to Katz.

They split the bill and pushed their way out onto Pennsylvania Avenue Southeast. The Capitol and the Supreme Court were a couple of blocks to the left. Wallace headed to the right and Katz fell in stride with him.

"So just 'cause the department needed to hire Negroes didn't mean our white brothers welcomed us with open arms. I got a dose right away. I got interviewed by this cracker Captain and when we done, he goes into the next room to talk me over with his boss. The door's open enough I hear him say 'A coon with a college degree; ain't that somethin'?'"

Katz winced.

"The shit never stopped. Tell me somethin', you ever pull traffic duty, man a crossing?"

"Yeah."

"How long you out there?"

"An hour."

"Then your relief comes, right?"

"Right."

"How'd you like to be out there for seven hours? In the snow? That's how long they left my ass out there." He punched out his arm and pointed, past Katz to the left. "Eighth and H, busiest fuckin' intersection in Northeast, last January."

Katz knew not to ask if he was serious this time.

"It was so bad, a white cop took pity on me. Guy named Blagdon, must have drove by three or four times, finally told me to get over to the curb, let me come in and sit with him, gave me some coffee. Boils me up all over again just thinkin' about it!"

They walked in silence till Katz heard Wallace blow out a long breath. He turned to see him shaking his head.

"Many a day I asked myself why I didn't just tell 'em to kiss my black ass right there and then and walk on out. But where I was going to go, man? Back to Greenville? No, they had me bought and paid for."

He tapped Katz on the arm and they hustled across North Carolina Avenue to beat the light. When they got to the other side, Wallace picked up the story.

"So they put me and Marcus together in a car, in Southeast of course, 'cause no white boy wanted to deal with all the crap goin' on there, and we settled in and we did a good job. There was a lot of drugs and assaults, rapes and murders here and there, but it was kiddie camp compared to the shit goin' on today. Anyhow, we're dealing with everything they throwin' at us in the station house and out on the street, we got each other's backs, and it's about as good as it's gonna get.

"And then comes December 27, 1959. Ten forty-three p.m."

183

He motioned to turn down Sixth Street. At D Street, Wallace stopped and nodded up to the corner ahead.

"That's South Carolina. You can see Sixth Street is one way comin' at us. We were drivin' up this way in Marcus' Lincoln, lookin' for a parking space so we could drop in at the Hawk. He got it used, a '56 Premiere, yellow, power steering, power brakes, beautiful. Kept it like new. He stops at the stop sign there but when we come through, this baby blue Caddy tears right through the stop sign at the left there on South Carolina. Marcus slams on the brakes but he skids into the guy, hits him just behind the driver side door and sends him spinnin' around and into the light pole."

He pointed at the pole on their side of the street.

"Marcus hops out and sees what this crazy nigger did to his car and he goes crazy himself. He runs up there, pulls this jackass out of his car and drags him over to see what he did. Whole hood's pushed right back up into the windshield, fender's draggin' on the ground, smoke and steam comin' up. I'm still in the car, man, dazed, watchin' all this through the windshield like it's a movie or something. Then the guy starts trying to twist away from Marcus, smackin' him on the shoulders, then upside the head, and so I pull my gun out of the glove compartment, my service gun, and I jump out my side and I yell at him 'Halt, man, stop right there. We're cops, man!' Don't make a shit to this guy, he's just about to rip away from Marcus so I grab him by the arm and yank him over to me. Then I cuff him on the head."

He swung his right arm down toward Katz' left ear.

"And blam! The gun goes off."

He stopped, the sweat popping off him like the gun exploded all over again right then and there. Katz stared at him wide-eyed, his throat dry.

"Then what, man?," he asked. "What happened?"

Wallace licked his lips, staring straight ahead at the empty intersection but seeing the Lincoln, the Caddy, the crazy nigger, and Marcus clear and sharp one more time.

"Bullet hit Marcus. Right in the eye, left eye. He goes down, blood bursting everywhere. Guy takes off. Then it's just me standing there, gun still in my hand, Marcus on the ground bleeding out. I kneel down next to him, try to stop the blood with the heel of my hand but it keeps pourin' out. Then, that's it. He's not breathin', he's cold. I know he's dead but I can't believe it. I can't. I try to wipe the blood off his face, give him mouth to mouth, but he's gone, man, gone."

"Holy shit!" was all Katz could say. The two of them stood frozen, one reliving the moment for the millionth time, the other trying to even imagine it.

Wallace dipped into his jacket for another cigarette. Katz tapped his arm and asked for one too to calm his nerves. Wallace lit them both, cool and steady again. He drew a deep drag and swallowed it all. Katz stifled a cough and puffed out a cloud.

"What'd they do to you?" he asked. Wallace shrugged.

"Inquiry, suspended -- with pay, thanks to the FOP crawlin' up their ass. In about five, six weeks, Board says it was an accident, so they put me back on duty."

"On patrol?"

"Shit, no, man. A nigger who shot his partner? Who they gonna stick with me? No, they found Mickey Mouse stuff for me to do around headquarters, filin', fillin' out reports, hopin' I'd make it easy on 'em and quit, but I wasn't goin' nowhere, man. So, finally, after months of that, I told 'em they were stuck with me so they might as well put me somewhere I could do 'em some good. So they make me a

185

plainclothes down in Anacostia. Black face helped there, see?"

He shrugged. "But that was okay with me, so everybody was happy."

"When was this?"

"Let's see, late '62, winter sometime."

"And when did you make Detective?"

"Last year. June '67."

"That's a long time on plainclothes, isn't it? You must've really liked it."

"Not that much. I started takin' the Detective exam in '64."

"Tough, huh?"

Wallace flicked his cigarette into the street.

"I took it and I flunked it four times in a row. Am I that stupid, man? Do you think I'm so stupid I couldn't pass the same fuckin' test four times in a row?"

"No, man. So what happened?"

Wallace reached back into his pocket, then seemed to think better of it.

"Where you parked, man?" he asked Katz.

"Back around the corner from the Hawk, on Third."

"I'm down that way too."

They walked almost the length of the block before Wallace went on.

"So here's how they pick you. Half the score is based on what your Sergeant says about you. The rest is on the tests."

"Your Sergeant screw you over?" Katz asked.

"No, he did right by me, but it was the multiple-choice test, every time. They print out a report that tells you how whitey did and how the Negroes did, okay? And every year, whitey does better and more whiteys gets promoted and more brothers don't. They use that test to keep us out."

186

"You really think that's what they're doing?"

Wallace stopped and looked at Katz like he was too stupid to tell time.

"Are you fucking serious, man? Of course, that's what they're doing."

"But you passed, right?"

"Yeah, the fourth time, after Sgt. O'Bryant got me in his study group."

"Who's that?"

"Tilmon O'Bryant? Detective Sergeant?"

Katz didn't recognize the name.

"He got a bunch of stuff together for us to study all about procedures and administration that I never knew even existed. Told us 'If we can study, we can compete'. So we studied and I passed, the fourth Goddamn time around!"

"That must've felt great."

"It would've the first time but, man, I'm the same cop I was four years ago except now I know some chickenshit regulations don't matter to no one anyhow. Why didn't they promote me then?"

Katz knew Wallace had only one answer to that. He bit his tongue but then thought if they were really partners, they had to be able to level with each other.

"Maybe you really do need to know the answer to those questions, Tom. If they're asking everyone the same questions, where's the prejudice?"

Wallace hacked out that harsh laugh again.

"You sound like the lawyer for the Goddamn MPD, man! That's exactly what he told us."

"Really?"

"Yes, really. You think the same way? Glad I know!"

They were at Third Street.

Wallace said "I'm down the block."

"I'm up this way," Katz said.

Wallace turned away without a word.

As Katz watched him disappear into the night, Jarvie's words flashed through his mind one more time. *You're thinking like a lawyer. He's thinking like a cop.*

It never meant more to him than right now.

32

They watched him reach into his inside jacket pocket, pull out a pack of Salems, shake one out, and light it. He stretched across the table to pull the ash tray nearer and flipped the match into it. He inhaled a long drag and swallowed every bit of it. He looked up at the clock over the window, then pulled in another deep drag.

Katz glanced over to Wallace, looking for some way to bring up last night, tell him he didn't know what he was talking about, ask him what his lawyer had to say about the test, even apologize if that would get them back on an even keel. But Wallace was as unreadable as ever, so he just asked "Ready?"

"Yeah," Wallace said. "Got your letter?"

Katz patted his right rear pocket.

"Okay. Once you play that out, I'll be right in."

"Then what? A little 'good cop, bad cop'"?

Wallace stubbed out his cigarette and stifled a laugh.

"Man, stop watching them movies. Just play off me, okay?"

Katz headed for the door.

"And don't make him think you think he had something to do with her gettin' shot. I don't want to hear from any more lawyers."

Katz gave him a tight smile and left. A few seconds later, Wallace watched him come through the door just behind Jerome. The big man stood up, towering over Katz. He laid his cigarette in the ash tray and offered his hand with a big smile.

"Jerome Terry. You can call me Jerry, Jerry Terry, Geri-Curl," he said, pointing to the shiny ringlets adorning his head. "I answer to all of 'em."

Katz shook his hand and held on to it.

"Jake Katz. Ring a bell?"

Katz felt Jerome's hand weaken for just a moment.

"No," he said. "Should it? Have we met somewhere?"

"No. But maybe you know my phone number? My address?"

"Sir, Officer Katz, you're losin' me here."

"A few weeks ago, my wife got a call from someone who told her I needed to keep my nose out of where it didn't belong or he'd do it for me."

"Okay."

Katz kept his eyes locked on the big man's eyes. If Terry didn't get it before, he got it now.

"Whoa now. You think that was me? No, no, no, sir, that's not Jerry's way. I'm just a nice big fun-lovin' good natured man, sir, got no enemies, don't want no enemies. Wasn't me, man, I promise you."

Katz released his hand and pulled the envelope from his pocket. He held it up so Terry could read "Chesapeake and Potomac Telephone Company" in the return address.

"You're sure about that?" he asked. "Want to think about it a little more?"

Terry reached over to the ash tray, knocked a long ash off his cigarette, sucked the rest of it down, and ground it into the ash tray before he answered.

"You think this guy was talkin' about you lookin' into Brenda bein' shot?"

"I do."

Terry shrugged.

"And why would you think that was me?"

"Because I talked to people who might've told you your name came up in the conversation."

"People, huh? What people?"

"Edward Jackson. Emmett Crowe."

Terry sat back down and thought a little while before he answered.

"Okay," he said, "let me say, right off, I can definitely see how you might think that way. I got it, perfectly understandable." He reached into his pocket for another cigarette then seemed to think better of it. "'Course, I can understand why someone might give you a call like that too."

"Really? Why is that?"

"I'm just supposin', you know, that if someone heard you'd been askin' questions about him, pryin' into his private life, tryin' to make him a suspect for somethin' he didn't do, he might not be too happy about all that. You can see that too, right?"

"So that's why you called me? Is that what you're telling me?"

Terry pointed at the envelope.

"Somethin' in there you want me to see? I mean, if I would've made a call like that, you think I'd make it from my own phone? Guy would have to be real stupid to do that, wouldn't he? You think I'm that stupid, you show me what you got and read it to me real slow-like, so I can figure it out."

The door flew open and Wallace burst through, panting from his sprint around the corner.

"Hey, I am so sorry, gentlemen. Traffic's a bitch out there. You Mr. Terry? I am a big fan of yours, sir, and so sorry for your loss."

Terry eyed him up and down.

"Who are you, brother?'

"Tom Wallace. I'm the detective working the case with Officer Katz."

"Whoa, now, how 'bout that? A brother makes detective in the MPD. Wow, they call you *Mister* Tibbs I bet, huh?"

Katz saw Wallace's neck muscles tighten. Terry must have too.

"Hey, I'm just jokin' with you, man. That's just Jerry, baby. Come on, sit down, join the party. Let's keep talking, talk about whatever you want."

Watching him cross behind Terry, Katz felt that for the first time he had some inkling of what it was like to be Tom Wallace day in and day out. Who was there for him, white or black? Why wouldn't he resent Katz? If it was me, I'd resent everybody. But Wallace showed him one more time who he really was. He slowly circled the table, sat down across from him, and threw open his notebook. He waited till Katz sat down to ask his first question.

"Can you tell me where you were when Miss Queen was shot?"

"Right behind her. I heard some commotion out there but I had no idea why or what was goin' on. We just kept doin' what we were doin'. I'll never forget it, second verse of 'Take Some Time Out For Love,' the Isley Brothers song?"

Wallace looked at him blankly.

Terry danced in his seat, holding his hands up high, twisting from side to side.

"'If your hands are tied and you just can't seem to get 'em free.' You know it? No?"

Katz knew it and loved it. "Cause your old tough boss won't show you no sympathy" slid through his synapses.

"Anyhow, I spin back around and there's Brenda layin' on the floor." He spread his hands, then patted his chest. "The blood was already comin' out in a big puddle. I kneeled down there and I yelled at her, 'Brenda, Brenda, honey, you okay?' but she didn't move. James tried to roll her over but I stopped him. I was afraid he'd kill her."

192

He was all the way back there now, his eyes rimmed with tears.

"I didn't know . . . If I had, I'd'a tried to do somethin'." He dipped into his jacket pocket and pulled out a handkerchief. "Sorry. Hit me all over again."

He wiped his eyes and shook his head, the curls bouncing in time.

Wallace waited for him a minute, then asked "Where did the shots come from?"

"Can't say. I was doin' that little spin move there, you know, with my back to the crowd? Turned back around, she was already down."

"Did you hear shots?" Katz asked.

"Yeah."

"How many?"

Terry shrugged. "Three? Four? I don't know. More than one's all I remember."

Wallace took his time writing notes in his pad.

"Did the two of you have a relationship?" he asked.

Katz thought he saw Terry pull back, but it was so quick he couldn't be sure.

"A relationship? You mean, was I fucking her?"

Wallace nodded.

"Yeah, I was. But, believe me, it was more like she was fucking me. We had an on and off thing for a long time, on mostly when she needed something that Walker -- Walker Thomas, her husband -- couldn't give her. Let's leave it at that."

Wallace kept his eyes on him, waiting for more, so Terry obliged.

"She had a way about her, made it hard to say no, you know what I'm sayin'? Woman has one hand on your dick and the other one on your wallet, you goin' along for the ride, okay?"

"So," Wallace asked, "what do you think happened that night? Accident, or something else?"

Terry leaned towards him.

"The truth? I think somebody took her out."

"Who?

"She had some nasty friends. Friends she couldn't keep away from, okay?"

"We saw her arms at the autopsy," Wallace said.

"Then you know. Maybe she was a little slow to pay up, more likely she told 'em to go fuck themselves. Whatever, guys saw their chance and they took it."

Right, Katz thought. Her dealers just happened to be standing in the crowd when the riot broke out and they were so smart, so quick, they decided to take her out just like that.

He must have been wearing his thoughts on his face again because Terry turned to him and said "Hophead motherfucker don't do a lot of careful planning, my man, just take advantage of whatever situation presents itself. Point the gun and go boom."

Katz was dying to challenge him but he made himself ask "Got any names? Anyone we can talk to about that?"

Terry threw up his hands and waved him off.

"Jerry don't travel in that crowd. Don't know 'em, don't want to know 'em."

Katz listened to Wallace wrap up the interview and watched him write down Terry's address and phone number in case they needed to talk with him again. Wallace stood up to say goodbye. Katz stayed where he was.

"Good luck to you guys. Hope you find whoever did this and burn 'em in hell."

When the door closed, Wallace sat back down and looked at Katz.

"You first," Katz said.

"Guy's fulla bullshit, no question about that."

194

"No question. A dealer got the bright idea to knock her off just like that?"

"That's crazy. But we're the ones getting' paid to figure out who did it, not him. We need to find this James, get his story."

"He still lives here."

"Okay, I'll look him up. You around all week?"

"Till Friday. I got a family thing up on Long Island."

"Okay, I'll get a good time and get back to you."

Wallace picked up his pad and turned to the door, then turned back.

"You think he called your wife?"

"Maybe. I don't know. If it's not him, I don't know who else would have."

Wallace held the door open for him.

"Another reason to talk to James."

33

She gave him the third degree about the stitches, the bruises, the hole in the haircut before he even got through the door. That he could handle. But it was the other question, the one he couldn't answer without lying to her face, that he dreaded the whole way up. When he pulled into the shul parking lot, he thought he had it made. But she was so about to burst, she popped.

"So, everything's all right with you and Lisa?"

"Mom, please, now? We're here."

"The last time, okay, she had to work, I understand. But today, a Saturday, she can't come? For your cousin's bar-mitzvah?"

"Mom, she's sorry. I told you, they needed her today. She just can't tell her boss no. It's not like that."

"I feel like I haven't seen her in a year. Or talked. Why is she never on the phone?"

"Mom, please, come on, they're waiting for us."

He jumped out of the car and came around to her side to open the door.

"Something's rotten in Denmark," she said. She pointed a finger up at him. "I know you, Jakelah. Don't tell me stories."

He pushed her finger down and pulled her up gently by the wrist. She was so light. His father always called her Zipporah, his little bird.

"There's nothing to worry about. If there was, I'd tell you. Come on."

He nudged her ahead, pretending not to hear her mutter "Tell me, right. Tells me nothing. Thinks I'm so stupid, I don't know. I know plenty," all the way to the door.

Cousin Jeffrey was his father's brother's kid. He was quite the card, though not nearly as funny as Uncle Hank and

196

Aunt Edie thought he was. Katz didn't feel particularly close to any of them, maybe because he always had trouble believing they were actually related. All of them were so different. Uncle Hank was as much of an egghead as his dad was a *shtarker*. He taught math at a community college and was famous in the family for making it to the last round of tryouts for the $64,000 Question. Jeffrey was already taller than Katz was, and probably twice as heavy, especially around the hips. "Baby Huey," his father called him and Katz smiled at the memory. Jeffrey knew every comedian's routine by heart and shared it with anyone at the slightest hint, which his parents made sure to drop at every family gathering. His rendition of "Hello Mudduh, Hello Fadduh" was especially famous, or notorious, depending on which side of the family you asked.

Katz' bar-mitzvah was a very low-key affair. So soon after her husband's disappearance, it was all his mother could do to make a chicken dinner at the house for Hank and Edie and Jeffrey, the only family members they had. It marked the end of his Jewish education and, except for the High Holidays, seders, and his friends' bar- and bat-mitzvahs, the end of his Jewish life. If he hadn't married a Jew, his mother would've ended the rest of his life but he did and she was happy about it, until now. He was never so happy to see a service start.

Except for an inexplicable yelp in the middle of his haftorah, cousin Jeffrey did very well. He was so confident, he lifted his eyes from the Torah to smile and even wink at his parents a few times. Katz followed his eyes to take a look at Uncle Hank, who was crying tears of joy, *kvelling* with pride.

Like all bar-mitzvah boys, Jeffrey concluded his part of the service with his take on a passage of the Bible. He picked Moses and the burning bush.

197

"Moses," he said, "came upon a bush that was burning, yet it would not consume itself. Then he heard a big booming voice. 'Moses, take off your shoes from off of your feet,' God said in his redundant way, 'for the land that you are standing upon is holy land.' Moses said 'What?' and God says 'Moses, do as I command you for I am your God!' so Moses takes his shoes from off his feet and steps into the burning bush -- and goes "Waaaaah!" and God says 'Ha! Third one today!' "

The place erupted. Even Katz had to laugh. His mother threw a hand up over her mouth. Uncle Hank gave Jeffrey a thumbs up. All the Rabbi could do was shake his head. It wasn't until the reception that Katz found out Jeffrey had cribbed the whole thing from a record by a comedian named David Steinberg.

The hijinks continued all through the party in the social hall. If Jeffrey wasn't leading a conga line of cigar-puffing thirteen year-olds across the dance floor, he was pouring salt into bottles of ginger ale and exploding with laughter every time the fizz rocketed out and soaked the table cloth. Quite the card indeed. For a change, Katz wanted him to go on and on, forestalling the inevitable conversation with his mother.

They were deep into the brisket and kugel when she turned to him. He pretended not to notice then called out "Jeffrey!" when he saw him approach the table with his beaming parents. He seemed to be limping. They came around to his mother first. She stood on tiptoes to hug him.

"Oy, Jeffrey! You were so good – and so funny! A regular Milton Berle!"

"Thanks, Auntie Fanny. I'm so glad you could come."

Uncle Hank was crying again. He hugged his mother.

"I only wish Sam, may he rest in peace, could have been here to see this."

"Me too, darling, me too."

Uncle Hank let her go and opened his arms wide to Katz.

"And you! Look at you, Mister Policeman! He's a regular – what – Adam Twelve? I don't know, I'm just so excited you're here. Where's your wife? Linda?"

"Lisa. I'm so sorry, Uncle Hank. She had to work at the last minute. She sends her love."

"Love? She needs to send me twenty bucks for the plate!"

"Hank!" Aunt Edie said.

"I'm kidding. I'm just kidding. I'm so happy to see you. We'll talk later at the house, okay? You'll fill me in on everything in Washington. What a time to be a policeman there!"

"It's interesting."

"I want to hear all about it. Fanny, you must be so proud of him!"

She managed a smile, then handed Jeffrey an envelope. He smiled and tucked it into his suit jacket pocket. He turned to move on, then winced in pain.

"Tatelah," she said. "What's wrong?"

"The rabbi kicked me."

"He what?"

"He kicked me, in the ankle, because I was going too fast. He told me he was going to do it but I thought he was kidding!"

"It'll just make him remember this wonderful day even longer!" Uncle Hank said.

"I wish you all the mazel in the world," Fanny said, reaching up to pinch his cheek before releasing him to let him collect the rest of his booty.

199

"I'm not too sure I really get Uncle Hank," Katz said when they sat down. "I'm never sure when he's kidding or not."

"He's a mentsch. What he says he means. Like your father, *alev ha shalom*. He never told me a lie."

The guilt was crushing him but he wasn't ready to give in.

"You don't know that. I bet there were a lot of things in his work he didn't tell you about. How would you know?"

"If he did, it was to protect me, so I wouldn't worry. But never about anything that mattered, about family. Never."

It was too much. He surrendered.

"Okay, you want to know? I'll tell you. She moved out."

Fanny threw her fork into her mashed potatoes.

"I knew it! I knew! When?"

"About six weeks ago."

"Six weeks? Six weeks and you don't tell me?"

"I was hoping it would work out and you'd never know."

She pressed her napkin to her mouth. Her eyes filled with tears.

"Fanny, are you all right?" Cousin Elsie asked from across the table.

Fanny nodded.

"I was just thinking of how much nachas Sam would have had being here."

At least Katz knew where he got his talent to lie so quickly.

"Excuse me," his mother said, and bolted from the table.

"I better go with her," Katz told Elsie and followed her out the doors and into a small circular sanctuary. She crumpled onto a bench, sobbing. Katz stood next to her, put a hand on her shoulder.

"And why?" she asked. "Why did she leave you?"

"She was afraid. She got a call one night while I was out from someone basically saying he was going to kill me."

Fanny fell back, terror-stricken.

"Kill you? Why?"

"I don't know. Really, I don't. I think it has something to do with a case I'm working on, someone trying to scare me off."

"*Vay iz mir!* Jakelah."

"It's nothing. It was that one time. Don't worry about it."

"Don't worry about it? Someone wants to kill you, I shouldn't worry about? Oy, this whole police business is craziness."

"Mom, please, don't start."

She shook her head, her right leg beating like a piston.

"You can't bring your father back. You know that, right?"

"Mom, please. I'm not doing it for him."

"No?"

"When I started, yes, that had something to do with it. But now, it's more than that. I like what I'm doing. I feel like I can make a difference, bring some justice to someone sometime."

"You couldn't bring justice to someone if you're a lawyer?"

"It's not the same. Plus, it's three years of school and then what? What if I don't like it? What do I do then?"

"You get a law degree, you can do plenty."

"I don't know. I'm still thinking about it."

Fanny thought about it a while too.

"And Lisa. When you find this person, she'll come back?"

Ten minutes ago, he would've told her yes, just so she wouldn't worry, wouldn't nag him. Now, he said "I think so. Maybe. I don't know."

"Why don't you know?"

"It's more than just the guy on the phone. That was just the trigger. We've been going round and round about law school, a baby, there's a lot up in the air."

"What does she say when you call her?"

"She doesn't. She won't talk to me."

"What?"

"Not since the day Bobby Kennedy got shot." Time to come clean on that too. "Before I saw you that morning, I drove to Cherry Hill to see her, be a comfort. She was crazy about him. But she ran away screaming. It was like I was some kind of curse, always bringing bad news. I don't know. Since then, she won't pick up the phone. Last week, I just stopped calling. There's no point."

Of everything he told her, this seemed to get to her more than anything. She balled her little fists up in front of her mouth and stifled a cry from deep inside. She couldn't stop the tears though and she leaped to hold him, wrapping her arms around his waist. He welled up himself but made himself stop. She didn't even try.

"Oh, my *tatelah*. What you've been going through."

"It's okay. It's not so bad."

They rocked together until she could calm herself down. She sat back down and patted the seat beside her. He sat and she held his hands.

"Jakelah, you've been honest with me, I'll be honest with you. Do I want you to go to law school? Yes. Do I want you to have a long and happy marriage with Lisa? Yes. Do I want to have a grandchild? Yes. But none of that

202

matters. It's what you want. All your father and I ever wanted was for you to be able to stand on your own two feet, do what you want with your life. That's why your *bobbe* and *zayde* came here for me and why your father's family came here for him. In America, you could be who you wanted to be. So that's it. Whatever you want, you should be."

"I know that," he said. "I just have to figure out what it is."

34

He stayed the night in his old room. She hadn't changed a thing. Ever since she threw out his baseball cards, she was probably afraid to.

The next morning, she made him salami and eggs and they talked about everything but Lisa, but law school, but the guy who wanted to kill him. She kept the conversation going with questions about everything else that was going on in Washington with that s.o.b. Johnson, his lackey the so-called big liberal Humphrey, that *ganef* Nixon. In the same breath that she lamented what the *schwarzes* did to Washington, she despaired over what they had to endure in this, the richest nation on earth. It was a *shonda*, a horrible shame on the country.

He drove her out to Longwood Gardens, where she'd never drive herself, so she could stroll among the flowers and bushes she loved so much. They walked hand in hand for a while, then sat on a bench, not saying a thing while she lifted her face to the sun and closed her eyes, letting the warm hand of God restore her, replenish her, cradle her being. When they were sitting more than they walked, he brought the car up and took her back home.

She wanted him to go while there was still plenty of light, but she didn't fight when he took her to the diner for a danish and some coffee on the way back. He went up to pack his things and by the time he came back down, she was sleeping soundly in the big chair by the door. He tiptoed past her but the creak of the screen door woke her up.

"Oy," she said, "I'm *takeh* exhausted. You wore me out."

"I'm going to head out now, mom."

"Can I make you something? You'll be hungry."

"We just had something. I'll be fine."

"Wait. You'll need something to *nosh* on."

"Mom --," he started, but she was already up and heading for the kitchen. By the time he came back in from the car, she was waiting for him with an Acme shopping bag.

"Here," she said. "There's grapes, a banana, an apple, a box of raisins, and a Tastykake with the white filling you love. Is that enough?"

"Mom, I'm not driving to Florida. It's three hours."

She pushed it into his arms.

"It's a long drive. You take it."

He bent down to kiss her goodbye. She hugged him as tight as she could.

"*Azai mit mazel*," she said. "You should always be with luck."

"Thanks, mom."

At the door, she clasped his free hand in both of hers.

"You're a good boy, Jake, and a smart one. I'm not going to start, don't worry. I just want you to always be well. And, please, no more keeping me in the dark, *forshtayst?*"

"I *forshtayst*. I'll let you know what's going on, good or bad."

"It should only be good. You drive safely."

He kissed her again and went out to the car. She waved goodbye and he headed out.

He was *takeh* exhausted too, from her, from the weekend, but maybe more than anything, from going over and over every if, and, and but about himself, Lisa, his life, her life, their lives. And here he was doing it again, the second he had a moment to himself. He made himself focus on what mattered more now:

Who killed Brenda Queen?

He took inventory of everything he knew, or thought he knew, starting with her.

She was a junkie.

She was an adulterer.

She was a ballbuster of the first order.

And she was about to jump to a different record company.

So what did all that say about who might have killed her?

A drug hit was preposterous but he couldn't rule it out.

Was it any less preposterous that Walker Thomas killed her for stepping out on him after so many years? Especially when he was queer?

Did he kill her because she was going to jump ship on him? But they were still married, so he'd get his cut anyhow.

Unless she had worked out some deal with the accountant that cut him out, and Walker killed him too. Or had him killed.

And how about greasy Jerry? He was sleeping with Brenda and he might have called Lisa but neither one of those things made him a murderer.

Unless Brenda was about to cut him out of something too. Money? Sex? Something else? He was a little coy about her dope habit. Was that part of what kept them together? Or was it something else he knew nothing about or couldn't put together?

Or was all of this speculation just a waste of time? What if it was just an unbelievable accident, a random bullet that found its way into her chest?

He was awash, overwhelmed by waves of uncertainty and doubt, suspicious of his own suspicions. Lisa pushed back into his thoughts, but the waves were even deeper there, so he punched up the radio and found the signal for TOP, just barely flickering in and out of the dead spot between Philly and Baltimore. The Nats were up 2-0 in the third against the Yanks. Must be a doubleheader. He was never so happy to listen to a ball game. He struggled to remember how happy he was as the Yankees climbed ahead and pummeled their way to a 12-2 demolition of the home team all the way back. A perfect complement to the 7-1 pasting they hung on them in the opener. At least some things in life were certain.

Trudging up the steps, he heard a phone ring louder and way longer than he would have hung on. Pushing through the door to the landing, he heard it blast from behind his door. He fumbled for the keys, cursing his clumsiness, hoping they'd hang on, reliving Lisa throwing the door open, seeing the horror gripping her face one more time.

He burst through the door and raced over to snatch up the receiver, his suitcase still in his other hand.

"Hello? Who is it?" he screamed into the receiver.

"Jesus Christ! Where have you been?"

"Who the fuck is this?"

"It's Floyd, man! What the hell's wrong with you?"

"Fuck!" Katz shouted, then winced, embarrassed at his show of nerves. He flipped the suitcase onto the sofa. It bounced off the cushion, banged onto the floor, sprung open, and spewed its contents across the room.

"Fuck!" he shouted again.

"That's it?" Floyd asked. "'Fuck?' Is that all you got?"

Katz muttered it one more time under his breath before falling back onto the sofa.

"I'm done. I'm sorry. What's up?"

"Your boy Wallace's been calling me every hour asking where you are."

"Why?"

"He won't tell me. Just says he needs to talk to you."

"Give me the number."

Floyd gave it to him. Katz dialed it and Wallace picked up on the first ring.

"This is Wallace."

"Hi. Jake Katz. Floyd –"

"Man, where you been?"

"Up in New York, and Philly. I had a family –"

"Hey, you know what? I don't really care. You in DC now?"

"Yeah."

"We got the gun."

"What gun? From the Howard?"

"Yep."

"How?"

"Garbage man found it. His grandma turned it in."

"How do you know it's the gun?"

"He found it in a dumpster behind the Howard. The ballistics guys cleaned it up and ran a test last week. The markings match the bullet the doc pulled out of Brenda."

"That's unbelievable."

"There's more. They found prints all over it, matched a street guy, a drunk who sleeps it off guess where?"

"The Howard."

"Good guess."

Katz tried to picture the guy sleeping it off the day he saw Brenda Queen with Scheingold but all he could pull up was the smell.

"Do we have him?"

"Yep. He was already in, on a public drunk. I talked to him this morning."

"And? Did he confess?"

"No. Said he had no idea how his prints got on it. Had no idea what he was doing in jail either."

"So what do you think?"

"I think you ought to talk to him, see what he tells you. We'll take it from there."

"Sounds good. Who do I ask for?"

"Delmott Winkley." He spelled it out for him. Katz grabbed a pen and wrote it out on the back of an empty Kool-Aid packet lying on the table.

Wallace signed off and Katz hung up. He looked at the clock. 7:25. He found his headphones and spun up WOL. He heard Arthur Conley ask him "Do you like good music? That sweet soul music?" He sang back "Yeah, yeah" and skipped down the steps to the street.

35

Ten minutes to eight the next morning, Katz pulled his cruiser into a lot on Independence, just around the corner from the entrance to the jail. He threw a salute to the guard at the top of the short tower just inside the barbed wire and shouldered his way through the knots of cops and lawyers clogging the walkway and the central foyer all the way back to the security office.

He asked to see Winkley. The clerk flipped through the sheets on his clipboard.

"Here he is." He scanned the sheet. "Illegal possession of a firearm. That's a new one."

"How do you mean?" Katz asked.

"Grandpa's in here every few weeks on a drunk count, maybe a disorderly, but that's the first time I've seen a gun charge. I know he likes the booze but I didn't know about the gunpowder. That's a bad mix, right there. Go on back and I'll get him down."

Katz grabbed a Miranda sheet and walked around the counter back to a pale green interview room, windowless except for the crud-encrusted square in the door. He threw his papers on the table and pushed his seat back. The metal tips scratched a sharp shriek on the floor. A flickering fluorescent bulb sputtered above.

At five after eight, the door creaked open and a guard nudged a gangly dark-skinned man into the room ahead of him. A faint musk of booze and sweat wafted Katz' way. He wouldn't swear he was the guy from that Tuesday at the Howard but he wouldn't swear he wasn't either.

Winkley hunched forward as he came through the door and listed slightly to his right before raising his cuffed hands to steady himself. The guard pushed past him.

"On or off?" he asked Katz.

"Off is fine."

The guard unlocked the handcuffs and pointed Winkley to the other side of the table. He fell into his seat with a loud grunt.

"Knock when you're done with him."

Katz nodded and waited till he left before turning to Winkley. He was licking his lips, eyes closed. His head fell forward, then lurched back. His eyes sprung open from the jolt. The fluorescent flashes exposed every pockmark and crevice that etched his hairless face. Patches of dark freckles clustered high on each check and below his rising hairline. His brown eyes swam in pools of red. If grandpa told him he was forty or eighty, he wouldn't've been surprised.

"Delmott Winkley?"

"Yes, sir. That's me."

"I'm Jake Katz with MPD."

"Pleasure to meet you." His eyes drifted shut, then fought to open.

Katz handed Winkley a pen and pushed the Miranda sheet across the table. He pulled a card from his wallet.

"I need to read you your rights," he said.

"Man, I know my rights. I'll talk to you, no problem."

"Still got to do it. You can sign when I'm done." When he finished his recital, Winkley signed and pushed the paper and pen back across the table. Katz flipped open his pad.

"I want to talk to you about the night Brenda Queen was shot at the Howard," he said.

Winkley's brow furrowed. He forced his eyes to focus on Katz.

"Didn't we talk about that already?"

"No, we didn't."

"Talked to someone."

"You talked to a detective, Mr. Wallace, about that, yesterday."

"There you go."

"I just want to go over what you told him and maybe ask you a few more questions."

"Okay. That's okay. What'd I tell him?"

Katz stifled a laugh. "I'd rather you tell me what you remember from that night."

Winkley nodded and licked his lips. He focused on a spot over Katz' head for a good long while. Katz pictured his brain struggling upstream against a torrent of vodka. Finally, Winkley said "She got shot."

"Right. And where were you when she got shot?"

He put his elbows on the table and massaged his temples with the heels of his hands. He shut his eyes tight and bared his teeth.

"Up in the balcony."

Katz pictured the hand-lettered "No Admittance" signs strung across each stairway up.

"I thought that was closed."

"It is," Winkley said, "except Mr. Crowe, he sometime make me go up there when a show's on."

"Why's that?"

"Need the seats, he say. I ten' to sprawl out, he say."

Now Katz knew: He was the guy. He'd have to tell Schein.

"What's so funny?" Winkley asked. Katz got his game face back on.

"Nothing, just thinking of Mr. Crowe telling you that. So where were you in the balcony that night?"

"Can't really remember one night from the other, you know. Mos' nights when I go up, I just lay down in the hallway there, back up behind the seats."

"So what did you see?"

212

"Nothin', till after she got shot."

"Did you hear anything?"

"They was yellin' stuff."

"Do you remember what they were yelling?"

He shook his head.

"No. I was tryin' to sleep. Tuck my head up under my arms, keep the noise out."

"Did you hear any shooting?"

"Yeah."

"What did you hear?"

"Shots."

"How many?"

His eyes closed. Katz waited. Until Winkley's head pitched forward.

"Mr. Winkley!"

Winkley's eyes popped open.

"How many shots did you hear? The night Brenda Queen was shot."

Winkley lifted his gaze again. Katz wanted to believe he was concentrating on the question.

"Some."

"How many's 'some'?"

"Four? Five? Mo'n two, I know that."

"Where did they come from?"

Winkley shook his head.

"Down below somewhere. Hard to tell." He stroked his chin. "Hard to remember."

"What did you do when you heard the shots?"

"I tucked myself in behind those seats good and tight till I didn't hear 'em no more."

"Then what?"

"I poke my head up and hear all this screamin' and yellin', even mo' 'n befo'. That's when I crawl down the walkway to the front of the balcony and I poke my head up

213

jes' a little till I can see over the edge to see what's goin' on."

"And what was goin' on?"

"I see everybody all goin' every which way and there this bunch a people kneelin' down up on the stage huddled 'round someone with they legs stuck out on the flo', a lady."

"Then what?"

Winkley's eyes widened and blinked rapidly. He lowered his gaze to meet Katz' eyes.

"I don't remember."

"Mr. Winkley, did Detective Wallace tell you we found the gun that fired the bullet that killed Brenda Queen?"

"You did? That's good."

"It is good. But did he tell you that your fingerprints were on the gun?"

Winkley's eyes widened more.

"What?"

"Your fingerprints are on the gun that killed Brenda Queen."

"No, that can't be right. I don't have no gun!"

"Someone found the gun in a dumpster behind the Howard and brought it in to us. It matched the bullet that killed her and it had your prints on it. How do you explain that?"

Winkley covered his ears and shook his head. His eyes welled red and wet.

"No, no, no. That can't be. I never killed no one. No one!"

"Then how did your prints get on the gun?"

Winkley pushed his chair back from the table and shot up, then fell back into the seat, sending it screeching across the floor and into the wall. The guard's face popped into the murk on the window. Katz held up a hand. The guard watched Winkley bury his face in his hands, then sit up straight and take a deep breath.

"You say I spoke to another po-lice?"

"Yes."

"What'd I tell him? Did I say I did it?"

The guard looked over to Katz. Katz flashed him the OK sign and watched him leave.

"Mr. Winkley, I'm trying to find out what you remember."

But Winkley's mind was running in a different direction.

"Is that why I'm in here? You all think I killed Miss Queen?"

"You're in on illegally possessing a gun right now."

"But I don't. I ain't own a gun forever, not since I was a punk kid."

"Then how did your prints get on it?"

He looked at Katz, stricken.

"I don't know. Did I shoot her?"

"Mr. Winkley, I don't know. That's why I'm here, giving you a chance to tell me, explain how your prints got on that gun."

"Maybe I did. Oh my God, did I kill that poor woman? Did I?"

He jumped out of his chair, knocking it over. He grabbed his head and screamed. The guard threw the door open and looked quickly over to Katz. Katz looked at Winkley, his arms wrapped over his head, quivering, his muffled sobs the only sound in the room. He looked back to the guard and nodded.

"We're done."

36

After his shift ended the next morning, Katz drove out to meet Wallace at his station house off Maryland Avenue N.E. The 9th precinct covered a huge swath of the District's most dangerous neighborhoods, sprawling from Capitol Hill to the Anacostia. Katz could conjure up a few good reasons and one real bad one why the department stuck him in the 9th. The conjuring stopped when he knocked on the door frame of Wallace's closet of an office at the back of the second floor. No door, no window, just a gray metal desk and file cabinet that seemed to squeeze him against the wall. Katz waved his way in through a cloud of mentholated smoke.

Wallace peered up at him through the fog.

"C'm'on in. I'd offer you a chair, except . . ."

"No problem," Katz said, and perched himself on the corner of the desk away from the ash tray.

"So, you talk to Mr. Winkley?" Wallace asked.

"I did."

"And?"

"I don't know, I really don't. He's either a heck of an actor or too blotto to remember anything. What do you think?"

Wallace stubbed out his butt and fired up another one.

"Same. I checked his rap sheet. It's a mile long, ten miles long, but there's no gun charge, nothin' violent at all, ever."

"Did you get a look at the prints and the ballistics?"

Wallace nodded.

"Looked solid to me."

"So where does that leave us?"

Wallace glanced at his watch. "Let's figure that out after we talk to James. Turns out he's in Memphis." He pointed back through the door. "Use the phone on the secretary's desk out there. We share a line."

Katz took the chair next to the desk and waited for Wallace to dial up the number and point to him. He picked up to hear James Jackson say "Hello?"

"Hello, Mr. Jackson," Wallace said. "This is Detective Wallace with MPD."

"Right. How are you, sir?"

"Good. Officer Katz is on the phone with me too. Do you have a little time to talk to us about the night Miss Queen was shot?"

"I do."

"That's good. How's Memphis this morning?"

"Hot, man, fryin'-egg-on-the-sidewalk hot. Goin' to be bad all week. That march gonna be a killer."

"What march is that?"

"Memorial for Dr. King on July 4, Thursday? Starts out on Beale St., then down to the Lorraine Motel, where he got shot."

"Right. You going?"

"Absolutely. Have to honor the man, you know?"

"That why you're down there?"

"Not just for that. Stax brought us down here to try to figure out what to do with us."

"Who's 'us'?"

"The Jacks. Me, Edward, and Jerome."

"I thought you were through with Stax," Katz said. "Didn't Warners grab you?"

"Yes sir, they did, till Brenda died. Then I guess they decided to cut their losses."

"What happened?"

"They killed the contract. Kept all the old stuff, of course, but let us go. We're down here working with Isaac and David, tryin' out a few things."

217

Katz couldn't resist. "Like what?"

"Like backin' up Carla Thomas."

Katz liked that. He heard "B-A-B-Y" echo in his ears and tried to picture the Jacks syncopating behind her. "That's pretty cool" died on his lips when he caught Wallace's glare through the doorway.

"So," Wallace said, "let's talk about that night at the Howard. Just go through it. Tell us what you saw."

"I didn't really see all that much, you know, with the lights and all? I could hear a lot of babble and yellin' out there but the band kept on playin' so we just kept on doin' our thing, you know?"

"Right," Katz said.

"We were crankin' through 'Take Some Time Out For Love,' you know, the Isleys' song? And I was facin' the band when I hear these pops – pop, pop, then another pop, pop – and when I spin back around, Brenda's down there, blood runnin' out her head. I saw it and I still can't believe it, you know?"

"Do that again? What'd you hear?" Wallace asked.

"Two pops kinda quick, you know, pop, pop? Then a little pause, then another pop, pop."

"Four shots in all?"

"That's how I remember it."

"You said you were facing the other way but can you remember where they might have come from? Did all of them come from the same direction?"

"Man, I can't help you on that. You gotta remember, the band was playing right in our ear, we were singin', Brenda was singin'. Lotta noise all over and those pops just popped outa nowhere."

"Any chance they might've come from up in the balcony?" Katz asked.

James waited a while to answer. Katz pictured him pantomiming his dance, like Jerome did.

After a minute, he said, "I don't know, man. I want to help you but I'd just be makin' something up, you know?"

"What happened after you saw she was shot?"

"Oh, man, Edward and Jerome and me, we were on our knees, beggin' her to open her eyes. Watty -- Irwin C. Watson, the comedian? -- he was down there and Mr. Crowe, the GM, he come up. It was just crazy, crazy horrible." Another pause. "She was family too, you know?"

"Right," Katz said. "We talked to Edward."

"She had her problems, you know, like all of us, but she was a good woman, and a hell of a singer, and she was takin' us with her to the top, man, to the top. It was all openin' up for us, then, then – aw, what's the point, huh? What's the point even talkin' about it?"

Wallace put a hand over the receiver to ask Katz if he had anything to ask but before he could answer, James had his own question.

"Hey, you answer me somethin'?"

"What's that?" Wallace said.

"You got some idea by now who might'a done it?"

Wallace said "We're still workin' it, talkin' to everyone who might've been in a position to see somethin', know somethin'."

"Talk to Mr. Crowe then, I guess, huh?"

"Yeah. Anybody else you can think of?"

"Guys in the band, you talk to them?"

"Not yet. If you've got some names, we'll find 'em."

"I can get 'em for you, from Charlie Hampton, the band leader. The only other person I know'd be there'd be old Delmott but I don't suppose he'd have much to tell y'all."

"Delmott?" Katz asked. "You mean Delmott Winkley?"

"Yeah. You know him? You boys done your homework if you talked to him."

"How do you know him?" Wallace asked.

"Shit, every time we in town, I sit and talk to him, try to get him straight. Never make a bit a' difference but I don't mind. Passes the time for both of us."

"How long have you known him?"

"How many years we been playin' the Howard? Six, seven? He's always there, man."

"We checked out his record," Wallace said. "Looks like a lot of public intoxication, loitering, but nothin' violent. That your take too?"

"Winky? Violent? Never. Hold on. You thinkin' Winky might'a shot Brenda?"

"We got some evidence that points that way."

"That's crazy, man, pure crazy. He wouldn't hurt a fly. The guy's a drunk, no question 'bout that, but he's a sweetheart, man, not a mean bone in his body. You barkin' up the wrong tree on that one, fellas, I promise you that."

Wallace put his hand back over the receiver. "You got anything else?"

Katz shook his head no.

"Okay then, James, I think that's all we got for you today. Can I give you my phone number so you can let me know who was in the band that night?"

"Yes, sir."

Wallace gave him the number, thanked him for his time, and hung up. Katz came back into the office and took his perch again.

"What do you think of this Stax thing?" he asked.

"What do you think?"

"Well, let's think about this. Brenda gets killed and Warners doesn't want them anymore, so Stax gets them back."

"Without Brenda," Wallace reminded him. "Why would they want to kill the golden goose?"

"Maybe making money wasn't the point. Maybe someone at Stax wanted to kill her just to stick it to Warners."

"Could be," Wallace said. "Spite's one hell of a motivator for some people. But how does that account for Winkley's prints all over the gun that killed her? He's not who I'd pick for a hit man, that's for sure."

"You really think he did it?"

"You didn't answer my question."

"I don't know. Maybe he found it on the street somewhere and threw it in the garbage and just doesn't remember. And who knows how long it was there? If it was more than five minutes ago, he wouldn't remember anyhow. There could be a lot of explanations, right? Maybe there are other prints on there we don't have on file."

Katz had time to think while Wallace popped out a Kool, flicked a tall blue flame off his lighter, held it to the tip, and drew in a good half-inch of tar and wintergreen before letting it out along the wall behind him.

"Maybe we ought to check out the Stax angle a little more."

"I like the way you think," Wallace said, "'specially cause it gives me a good reason to go on down there an' enjoy a little of that Memphis Soul Stew on July the 4th."

"You really think they'll let you go?"

Wallace squinted up at him through the smoke. "I believe you makin' what the lawyers call a unwarranted supposition there, Officer Katz."

"What's that?"

"That I'm gonna ask anybody to let me."

"Why wouldn't you?"

Wallace rolled his eyes.

221

"They only goin' to tell me no, man. What's the worst that's gonna happen? They don't pay my voucher?"

He shook his head and flicked a long ash off the end of his cigarette.

"I'd rather call it a vacation than give 'em the satisfaction of getting' in my way one more time."

37

Katz had never been up to the third floor of headquarters. Coming out of the stairwell, he was amazed to see the crowd of humanity teeming before him. Lines at the counter ran ten deep or more. There were no chairs so people sat against walls wherever they could find space. Mothers yelled after their children. Almost everyone was black.

Katz picked his way through the lines in search of 3061, the criminal records room. He found it three doors down the hall and went in. The counter there separated him from the same room full of files behind the counter he just passed. Everyone on the other side of the counter was white.

A pleasant middle-aged woman in civilian clothes rolled her chair up to meet him.

"Good morning, dear. Who you looking for?"

"Winkley. Delmott Winkley."

He spelled it out for her and she wrote it down on her yellow pad below a long list of crossed-out names.

"Is he in or out or don't you know?"

"In. What's going on out there, by the way?"

"The circus? It's in town every day. They all need clearances for jobs, taxi cab licenses, what have you. The ones waiting are the ones who've been here before, you catch my drift. Come on around and take a seat down there," she said, pointing out an empty chair on her side.

She left to get the file and was back by the time he sat down. She made a show of needing two hands to lift it and let it drop on the counter with a whack.

"Don't think *he*'ll be driving a cab any time soon. Just put your John Henry on the signout form inside there and you're all set."

Katz thanked her and turned the front page of the folder. He scribbled his initials below Wallace's. Winkley's rap sheet lay on top of what looked like four inches of paper. He took his time scanning it for anything with a weapon. Except for the current charge, the codes were all the same: public intoxication, loitering, disorderly conduct, failure to move on. The first one was dated December 2, 1929. They rolled by at a clip of five or six a year, except for a gap between 1939 and 1946.

Katz pulled the papers off the prongs and set them face down on the counter. He turned over the first arrest report. The type was smeared and faded but he could make out Winkley's date of birth -- February 18, 1905. That made him 24 the first time he was arrested and 63 today. Place of Birth, Clarksdale, Mississippi. From what Katz could read, he got in a fight over a pool game at a bar on Columbia Road. Released on his own recognizance.

He flipped through the back pages a little more quickly until he came to the reports for 1946. Caught urinating on private property up on Cathedral. This one had a handwritten bio sheet. Winkley checked Yes for Military Service and wrote "Army. Infantry. 1939-1944" next to it. Next to Place of Employment, he wrote "None."

The drunk charges came more frequently through the fifties. He was almost always out on his own recognizance, sometimes having to post $10 or $20 bail. Still no sign of a gun.

Katz picked up a bigger stack and turned it over. June 4, 1963. Sleeping on the sidewalk at 7th near Florida. August 1, 1963. Public intoxication, 7th and T. He flipped back to a December 1962 report. Another intox, at 7th and R. The reports putting him in the vicinity of the Howard started in 1961. He flipped forward to '64.

Now the charges were the same but the bail amounts started getting higher: $100, even $500. The hearing commissioners must have gotten tired of seeing him in and out and tried to get him some time to sober up at the jail. Didn't seem to work, though. He kept making bail. But now it wasn't his name on the Posted By line. He strained to read the ragged, awkward signature. Looked like Lillian something.

He flipped forward to the next one. February 18, 1965. Must have been celebrating his birthday a little too hard. Lillian bailed him out again. This time he could make out the last name. Crowe.

He flipped to the next one, then froze.

Lillian Crowe. Emmett Crowe. Leelee Crowe.

His hands trembled so hard he couldn't turn the pages without making himself concentrate on the edge of every sheet. Every arrest for the last four years, Leelee bailed him out.

He pushed the papers away from him. The dots were out there now, he just had to connect them. Delbert's prints were on the gun that shot the bullet that killed Brenda Queen. Delbert slept his drunk off at the Howard every day. Every time Delbert got busted, Lillian Crowe bailed him out. Lillian Crowe's uncle Emmett ran the Howard. Brenda Queen was shot at the Howard.

He slid the papers back on the prongs and took the file to the counter lady.

"Find what you were lookin' for?" she asked.

"I'm going to find out," he said.

38

Back at the 6th, Katz called Wallace's hotel in Memphis. The operator connected him to his room. The phone rang for a minute before she got back on the line.

"No one's answering. Do you want to leave a message?"

"Try it one more time please?"

The click of the transfer cut off her sigh. This time, Wallace picked up right away.

"Hello?"

"Hey, it's me, Katz."

"Damn, man. I was on the shitter, thinkin' what kind of fool is calling me at 8 o'clock in the morning? Now I know."

Katz looked up at the wall clock. 9:04.

"Sorry about that. I didn't know you were an hour behind us."

"This better be good."

"It is. I went through Winkley's file this morning. For the last four or five years, he's been getting bailed by Lillian Crowe."

"Yeah, so? Who's Lillian Crowe?"

"I think she's Emmet Crowe's niece."

"The Howard guy?"

"Yeah. I saw her up there once. He called her Leelee. I think it's the same person."

"You think."

"She works the candy counter for him, probably does whatever he says, including bailing out Winkley."

"'Why you say that?"

"She's a little off."

"'Off'. She a retard?"

"I don't know. I just think it's a good lead worth talking to her about."

"So that's where we are on this, huh? Talkin' to a retard about a drunk?"

Katz took the point and resented it.

"You got something better?"

"Not yet, but I'm still workin' it. There's a lot of spiteful people down here but not the way we talked about it."

"How do you mean?"

"The guy that owns Stax, named Jim Stewart? After he got screwed by Atlantic grabbin' all the old stuff, he turned around and sold what was left to Gulf and Western, for less than what Atlantic woulda paid him, just to fuck 'em over."

"Gulf and Western? What's an oil company know about soul music?"

"Probably nothin' but he wasn't gonna let Atlantic have it no way. Would've given it to the KKK for nothin' before he did that."

"So where does that leave us?"

"I got a few more people to talk to. Plus the ribs are pretty damn good down here, so it'll be another couple days before I get back. Figure Monday."

"How was the march?"

"You didn't hear?"

"No, what happened?"

"It was wild, man. Hadn't gone two blocks before some kids started throwin' bricks through some windows and the police come chargin' right in after 'em. I never even moved a step way back where I was. Soon as I heard what was goin' on, I got out of the line and headed back to the hotel, watched the rest of it on TV."

"Wow."

"These cops down here, they love that shit. Ain't seen one brother in a uniform since I been down here. Every time I show my badge, they look at me like I stole it or got it out of a cereal box or somethin'."

"I'm sorry, man. That must be tough."

"Oh, one more thing, The guy I told you about, Jim Stewart, that owned Stax?"

"Yeah?"

"He's white, you know that?"

"No."

"Man. You people don't leave us nothin'."

Katz still didn't know him well enough to know if he was joking or not so he kept his mouth shut. The click on Wallace's end told him the conversation was over anyhow.

39

The next morning Katz was up before dawn even though he knew Floyd wouldn't be calling him for hours. By 7, he had practically memorized the box score of the Nats' 8-4 win over the White Sox. Epstein's three-run shot in the second gave them a 6-2 lead and Coleman went the distance for the win. A whopping 3,271 rooted the home team on. He was on his second pass through the wedding announcements when the phone finally rang a little after 9.

"Floyd?"

"Yeah. I got him."

"Is he coming?"

"He's coming, but he ain't happy about it."

"What'd he say?"

Floyd did his best Stepin Fetchit impression. "'Why I got to waste my time comin' downtown to see a bunch of pictures? I told you all I know already, blah, blah, blah."

"What'd you tell him?"

"What you told me to tell him. We got a couple of suspects but we need him to tell us if he recognized any of them from the Howard."

"When's he coming?"

"11. He told me how busy he was. I told him 'I was there. You're not so busy.'"

"Call me when he gets there."

By the time the phone rang at 11:06, his cruiser had been idling at the curb for half an hour.

"He's here."

"I'm going up now. Keep him as long as you can."

40

Emmett Crowe was not a happy man and he let Floyd know it every time he turned a page.

"This is some bullshit, man."

"I heard you the first hundred times."

"The fuck I know who shot her?"

"Just tell me any faces you might know from the Howard. People in the crowd, someone who used to work there, someone who might've had business with you, or her, or --"

"Yeah, yeah. I heard you the first hundred times too."

Floyd did a slow burn but shut his mouth before he said what he was thinking. Crowe turned the pages more quickly, digging for the finish line.

"Mr. Crowe, take your time, all right? You're not even looking at half those guys."

"I'm lookin'. I see 'em. You think if I study 'em real hard, light's gonna pop on? If I see someone I know, I'll know it? Ain't that hard to figure out."

He muttered his way through the last page and slapped the back cover shut.

"All a bunch a strangers. Never seen a one of them. Been a pleasure."

He stood up to go but Floyd laid a heavy hand on his arm.

"We're not done."

He slid a second book down from the far end of the table and pushed it in front of Crowe. "We need your help here. Take your fuckin' time and give it to us."

Crowe looked down at the book, seething. Floyd took his pleasure in watching a vein swell and throb across the old man's forehead. Crowe took a deep breath, then another one, then slapped the book open.

41

Katz couldn't help himself. He ran the siren and the flashers the whole way up New York Av and 7th Street. He pulled the car around onto Wiltberger Street and looked at his watch. 11:15.

He yanked at the front door and it opened. He knew Crowe was with Floyd at HQ but still he stood and waited a minute to hear if any footsteps were heading his way. When he heard nothing, he headed into the theatre, then left to the closest stairway to the balcony. He stepped over the chain and tiptoed his way up to where Winkley told him he usually slept, then down the steps to the railing where he said he was that night. He let his eyes adjust to the darkness, then crawled back up the steps, reaching under each row of seats on both sides to see if there was anything that might confirm his story, or yank it out from under him.

At the top, he reached under the last row and felt a glass bottle. When he reached for it, he heard it clink against something else. He crawled around to the landing and pulled out one bottle, then a second, then another. His hand stuck to each one. He pulled them close to read the labels. Two Night Trains and a Thunderbird. The odor of the carpet triggered his memory of that afternoon down below. Delbert wasn't lying. About this anyhow.

He stood up and looked down at the unlit stage. He couldn't see the lip but he could see the back. He saw something move in front of the rear curtain and squinted to bring it into focus. It was a heavy black girl lying on the stage, rolling on to her side, facing him. It was Leelee.

He stood transfixed, afraid to scare her by calling out. She leaned on her left arm and hunched forward over something, her right hand moving busily over whatever it was. He tiptoed back down the stairs to the top of the aisle.

She didn't notice him at all. He walked slowly down the aisle and came to a stop at the front of the stage, maybe thirty feet from where she was lying. Her hair was natural and untamed, coiling out in all directions. She didn't lift her head. He could see now that she was coloring something in a book.

She lifted her head to look at him and said "Hello."

"Hi," he said. "Can I come up and talk to you a little bit?"

She shook her head yes and went back to her coloring. He came up the steps at the left. In the dim light, he couldn't see if Brenda's blood still stained the floor. He crossed over to Leelee. Her pudgy face shone with innocence. He twisted his head to see she was coloring Casper the Ghost a dark blue.

"That looks nice," he said. "I like blue."

She looked up at him and took in his uniform, then went back to her coloring.

"You a policeman?"

"I am."

"Do you know the policeman on TV who goes 'The facts, ma'am, just the facts'?"

"I know who you mean but I don't know him. He works in Los Angeles. I work here in Washington."

"I like him."

"Me too. Can I ask you a few questions?"

She nodded yes and kept coloring. He pulled his pad out of his rear pocket and flipped it open.

"First of all, I want to make sure I get your name right."

"It's Leelee."

"How do you spell that?"

"Capital L-e-e-l-e-e."

"That's a nice name. Is it your real name?"

233

She shook her head no.

"It's Lillian. L-i-l-l-i-a-n. But everyone calls me Leelee."

"Can I call you Leelee?"

She shook her head yes.

"Thanks. What's your last name, Leelee?"

"Crowe. Like the bird with an 'e' at the end."

"Leelee Crowe. Got it. That's a very nice name."

"Thank you."

"And how old are you?"

"Twelve," she said and held up the page she was working on.

"Wow," he said. "That is beautiful. You should be an artist."

She turned the page to another picture of Casper and a bigger ghost sailing through the sky.

"What color should I do them?"

"Hmm," Katz said, "how about red?"

"A red ghost? No! How about yellow?"

"Yellow. You're absolutely right. A yellow ghost is much friendlier than a red ghost."

She reached into the crayons scattered on the floor in front of her, then held up a yellow crayon as high as she could.

"There you go," he said. "Casper the Yellow Ghost."

"Casper the Yellow Ghost!," she laughed and started filling him in.

♦ ♦ ♦

"No one, okay?" Crowe said. "Happy now?"

"Delirious," Floyd said. "Take a breather. I'll get the next one."

"Next one? The fuck, man. I got a business to run."

234

"Business'll wait. Stretch your legs. I'll be right back."

"I got to take a shit. That okay?"

Floyd had to take one himself.

"I'll walk you back there."

He led him out to the hallway and down to the corner. He pushed open the Men's door and followed him in.

"You gonna sit here with me too?" Crowe asked.

"Take the last one. I'll be out here waiting for you."

Crowe swung the door open and pulled it shut behind him hard. Floyd heard the lock latch and waited till he heard the old bastard's pants fall before he took the stall closest to the door. He really needed to take a crap. It didn't take long to get things moving. Christ, he thought, that's the crosstown bus down there. He reached for the toilet paper then saw black pants and shoes run past him and heard the door to the hall smack open.

"Hey!" he yelled. "Get the fuck back in here!"

He yanked his pants up with one hand and unlocked the door with the other. He waddled into the hallway just in time to see Crowe running down the steps towards the street.

"Come back here, you old fucker!" he yelled but by the time he pulled himself together and got to the door, the old fucker was nowhere in sight. Floyd raced back to the mug book room and threw open the door.

"Where's a fucking phone book?" he screamed.

♦ ♦ ♦

Katz heard a phone ring from the direction of Crowe's office. He waited to make sure it kept ringing. When it cut off in mid-ring, he asked Leelee, "Do you know a man named Delbert?"

Leelee nodded yes.

235

"Delbert Winkley?"

"He's my best friend."

"Really? How did he get to be your friend?"

"We play."

"What do you play? Does he help you color?"

"No!" she laughed. "We play card games."

"Like what?"

"Umm, Go Fish. War."

"That sounds like fun. Do you ever see him anywhere else?"

"Sometimes. At the jail."

"Why was he at the jail?" he asked.

"I don't know. Daddy gives me money and I take it to the man at the desk and then he comes out."

"What's your daddy's name?"

She looked up at him, eyes wide.

"I'm not supposed to tell anyone. It's a secret."

"Your daddy's a secret?"

She nodded yes.

"I only told one other person and she wound up dead."

A cold chill grabbed Katz' chest and froze his arms.

"Who was that?" he managed to get out.

Leelee plucked at strands of hair drooping over her forehead.

"Brenda," she said. "She was nice. She always let me brush her hair, the kind that doesn't grow on your head?"

"A wig?" Katz asked.

Leelee nodded again, then reached out for another crayon.

"When did you tell her about your daddy?"

"The same day she died."

Katz knelt down next to her and whispered in her ear as softly and as sweetly as he could.

"You can tell me daddy's name, Leelee. I'm a policeman. I won't tell anyone. I promise."

She shook her head.

"I don't want you to be dead."

"How about if I guess? That way you wouldn't have to tell me. Can I guess?"

She sat back on her legs, staring at him.

"Is Mr. Crowe your daddy?"

She kept her eyes on the red crayon in her hands, rolling it over and over.

"That's all right," Katz said. "You don't have to tell me his name. Can you tell me your mommy's name?"

"Mommy."

"Is she Daddy's wife?"

She nodded, then looked up and put her finger to her mouth.

"And his sister," she whispered.

A surge of vomit rocketed up Katz's throat. He gasped for air to keep it down.

He heard Leelee yell "Daddy!"

He turned to see Emmet Crowe level a pistol at his face.

"You sick fucker," Katz said.

Crowe was halfway down the middle aisle. He kept the gun trained on Katz but talked to Leelee.

"Girl, go on back to Daddy's office and lock the door. Now."

"Daddy, don't hurt the policeman."

"Now, Leelee!"

She pushed herself to her feet and ran as fast as she could down the steps to the left. Crowe waited till he heard the door close.

"I told you that bitch had it coming to her," he said.

"Why? Because she knew about you and Leelee?"

237

"No. Because she was blackmailing me about it."

"What?"

"Goddamn Leelee told her that night, right before the show started. She comes back and tells me she knows all about it but she'll keep it to herself for my share of the take. Goddamn bitch, she wasn't making enough from screwin' everybody else? She had to take my nut too?"

"So you decided to kill her?"

"I wanted to but I wasn't planning on it -- till that riot broke out. As soon as I saw 'em comin' through the doors, I ran back to my office and grabbed the gun out of the desk. I ran back up the aisle over there," he nodded his head to the right, "and I was ready to plug anyone I saw tryin' to bust the place up. Then I hear those shots ring out from the back and it just hit me, like a bolt of lightning. This was my chance. I faded back into the corner and I drew a bead on her and I waited for the next shot and soon as I heard it, pow! She went right down and I thanked Jesus and Dr. King and all those fuckers in the lobby all the way back down to my office. I threw the gun back in the desk then ran up on the stage to see what had happened to poor fucking Brenda."

"How did Delmott's prints get on the gun?"

"Next morning, he's sleeping down front like always. I wiped it down, carried it out there in my gloves and pressed his hand all over it."

Katz shook his head in disgust.

"It was an insurance policy, man." Crowe said. "I wrapped that thing in a paper bag and stuffed it down the bottom of the dumpster. Never thought anyone'd find it in a million years. But if they did, well, what's the worst that could happen? Delmott get three square meals and a bed every day for the rest of his life? Step up for him."

"You frame a guy for murder and you're doing him a favor? You're too much, man."

"You know what? I'm tired of talking with you."

He cocked the revolver. Katz watched the barrel rise to stare him in the face. He'd never get his own gun out on time. He needed to keep the conversation alive to keep himself alive.

"Why'd you even put it in my head that she might have been murdered? Why not just let me figure it was a wild shot from the crowd and close the case?"

"Gave you too much credit, that's why. Figured one of you knuckleheads would find out enough to start thinkin' somebody put that bullet in her on purpose. Just wanted to make sure that when you did, you started lookin' in all the wrong directions.

"What're you going to tell Leelee, huh? What happened to the nice policeman?"

"That's somethin' you won't have to worry about. We done now, Officer. Bye bye."

He leveled the gun at Katz' chest. Katz heard it go off but didn't see a flash. He saw Crowe teeter towards him, then fall under the lip of the stage. He ran forward and heard footsteps running towards him. He stopped and saw Floyd charging down the aisle, pistol in his raised hand. Katz watched him kick the gun out of Crowe's hand, then kneel on his back. Floyd put his fingers on Crowe's neck, then rolled him over. A dead man's eyes looked up at Katz, frozen forever in disbelief.

August 28, 1968

42

He sat on the edge of the bed and tugged Lisa's letter out of its fat manila envelope for probably the fiftieth time. More a diary than a letter, she stuffed it with hundreds of random jottings about him, her, them, from the day Bobby died until the day she mailed it. He sifted through the welter of stationery, index cards, note paper, newspaper and magazine articles, greeting cards, all bearing her jagged handwriting, sometimes scratching down the margins and onto the back, in pencil, pen, and magic marker, red, blue, black, and green. Some of it was a love letter, how much she missed him, adored him, wanted to be with him forever. But then came the if only's, the regrets, the anger, the fears, over and over the fears, the pleas that he only understand and change for her sake, his sake, their sake.

At the top of the pile, probably after Anne Weiss let her know that the bad guy was dead and he was still alive, the tone softened, the strokes calmed down, the cry for change melted to a plea to forgive. He couldn't keep himself from reading the one on top one more time. Hallmark supplied the rose on the front and the 'I Love You Forever' inside. Lisa supplied the rest.

"My sweet Jake," she wrote, "I wrote all these to myself, not knowing if I would ever have the nerve to show any of them to you. But after Anne called and gave me the news and I cried -- tears of joy -- all day and night, I knew I had to send them to you because I didn't know any better way to let you know how much I love you and miss you. My life has been so empty and such a mess without you. I hope you know that now and I hope even more that you'll have me back. I love you and can't wait to hear from you and see you soon. Love, Lisa"

The heavy knock on the door startled him, sending the pile cascading to the floor. He slid it under the bed and dashed out to the living room just as Floyd let himself in.

"Hey," he called to Katz. "Where's everyone else?"

"You're first," Katz told him. "Didn't think you were this interested in politics."

"There's beer, right?"

Katz disappeared into the kitchen and came back with two quarts of Carling Black Label held high. He handed one to Floyd and waved him onto the sofa, then walked over to turn on the TV. Once he got a picture, he turned the dial to 7 and yanked the rabbit ears around till he got rid of the zebra stripes and they could clearly see cops wading into a crowd, swinging their batons at kids, pummeling them on the ground. The only sound was Howard K. Smith telling them what they were watching but they both heard the screaming and the shrieking, the sirens, the frantic wall of noise that overwhelmed them last April on 14th St.

"They're still going?" Floyd asked.

"I don't know," Katz said. "I think this is from the other night."

Floyd watched a helmeted cop grab a hairy kid by his collar and swing him to the ground. The kid covered up but the cop brought his baton down on whatever was exposed, over and over again. Floyd nodded approvingly.

"Those guys know how to take care of that shit. Hit him again!" he yelled.

Katz shook his head but bit his tongue, honoring his vow to never say an unkind thing to or about Floyd as long as he lived. They watched the scene unfold until Howard K. came back to tell them what they just saw.

"Where's Cronkite?" Floyd asked. "Why are we watching this buzzard?"

"Because he's got Buckley and Vidal coming on." If they were a country act, Floyd might've known them but they weren't so Katz explained. "They're political guys, one on the right, one on the left, and they hate each other. It's been crazy to watch."

The whole week had been crazy to watch. The Democratic National Convention was supposed to have been Humphrey's coronation but thousands of kids in the streets of Chicago were spoiling the ceremony. The last few nights, the country got to see the Chicago PD take back control in a way MPD never could or would. Howard K. let them know this was, in fact, today's carnage, erupting right after the Convention voted to reject the peace plank put forward by McCarthy and Senator McGovern of South Dakota.

It made Katz sick to watch but he couldn't turn away.

"So what do you hear?" Floyd asked.

"About what?"

"Man, don't be cute."

"Nothing. Wallace had his hearing today. He's supposed to call me."

"Either way's good for you, right?"

"How do you figure that?"

"He's cleared, you're happy. He's screwed, a detective job just came open."

"I don't want his job. You know that."

Floyd finished a guzzle and wiped his chin with the back of his hand. "Won't be his job. No way they stick you out there. You'll get your own office at HQ, view of the Capitol, the whole deal."

The door pushed open and Scheingold and Weiss came through. Katz pointed them to the kitchen and they came back with quarts in hand. Scheingold took a look at the tube and recoiled.

"You've got to get a better picture than that," he said and immediately began jerking the rabbit ears with his free hand. The diagonal lines subsided. Harry K's face sharpened.

"Perfect," Katz said. "Just stand there and keep holding it."

Scheingold let go and Harry K. blurred and weaved, then came back more or less in focus.

"Leave it, Schein," Weiss said. "He's less scary like that." He perched on the arm of the sofa next to Floyd. "So what'd we miss? Anyone else kicked to shit for being an American?"

Floyd shot him a look and started to straighten him out but the ring of the phone cut him off. Katz sprung to his feet and headed for the bedroom. He threw the door shut behind him and ran around the bed to pick it up.

"Hello?" he said.

"Well, hey there, my man."

It sounded like Wallace, but slower, blurrier, like a bad tape.

"Detective Wallace?"

"It's Wallace, all right, but you can drop the Detective now."

"Why? What happened?"

"Hold on. I'll read it to you. Don't want to get it wrong." Katz heard wood scrape, the jingle of glass, then a paper unfolding for what seemed forever.

"'Dereliction of duty', that's it."

"For what?"

"Let's see. Sorry, hold on. Okay, here we go, 'Going to Memphis, Tennessee, without permission to take part in a violent political protest and exposing a fellow police officer to unnecessary risk by his absence.' How's that? Sound pretty bad, huh?"

"That's horseshit. I told them exactly what happened. You didn't expose me to anything."

"You 'n me are square, man, don't worry 'bout that. We're cool."

"So what'd they do to you?"

"Bust me back down to patrolman."

"Are you kidding me?" Katz said. He couldn't believe it. The disciplinary process was a joke. Everyone knew that. When Schein's cousin filed brutality charges against him for punching his lights out, nothing ever happened to him. But they bust Wallace for this? He could think of only one reason why.

"But, hey, man," Wallace said, "I'm lookin' on the bright side."

"What's that?"

"I get to keep my office. Hah!"

Katz felt nauseous.

"You got railroaded, man. That's not fair."

He heard nothing on the other end.

"Detective? You there?"

Now he heard some humming, then the tinkle of ice in a glass. He waited till he heard the hum turn into Wallace's version of singing, a song he didn't recognize.

"What's that?" he asked.

"Hey," Wallace said, "you ever hear of a group, the Staple Singers?"

"Yeah, they're a gospel group, right?"

"Right, but now Stax is tryin' to make 'em a pop group, like regular soul music."

"How'd you hear that?"

"Seen 'em down there. Mr. Stewart let me sit in on a session."

"Is that what you were singing?"

"What?"

"You were just singing something. I couldn't hear it. Sing it again."

Wallace mumbled "Got to be some changes made," with an emphasis on the 'Got', then muttered it again, this time with the semblance of a tune behind it.

"Doesn't sound like a hit to me," Katz said.

"'People all over the world," Wallace went on, "they're watchin' every move we make, we fightin', somethin' somethin', our babies are callin', doo doo doo, Got to be some changes made'. It's a hell of a song, man. You got to get it. Staples Singers."

Katz didn't know whether to laugh or cry.

"I'll get it, definitely. But, listen, can you appeal this thing?"

"Man, there ain't no use."

"No, there is, there has to be. I'll testify for you."

A whoop went up in the living room. Scheingold threw open the bedroom door.

"They're on, man! Buckley and Vidal!," he said, then ran back to his seat.

"You got company, man?" Wallace asked. "I'll go."

"No, no, don't go. Let's talk about this."

It took a couple of seconds for Wallace's sleepy, distant voice to come back on the line.

"That's a hell of a record, man. You get it."

This time he was gone. Katz cradled the phone and hung his head until Schein screamed at him again.

"You're missing it, man! Vidal's on fire!"

He made himself go out and watch. Vidal was talking.

"There are many, even in the United States, who happen to believe that the United States policy is wrong in Vietnam and the Viet Cong are correct in wanting to organize the country in their own way politically. This happens to be

246

pretty much the opinion of Western Europe and many other parts of the world. It's a novelty in Chicago. That is too bad but I assume that the point of the American democracy --"

Buckley cut him off.

"And some people were pro-Nazi, too, some people were pro-Nazi."

"Shut up a minute," Vidal said.

"Ow!" Schein yelled.

"No, I won't," Buckley said. "Some people were pro-Nazi. I know you don't care, because you don't have any sense of identification --"

"As far as I am concerned," Vidal said, "the only sort of pro- or crypto-Nazi I can think of is yourself,"

"Oh shit!" Weiss said.

Howard K. tried to restore order. "Let's not call names," he said. Buckley must not have heard him.

"Now listen, you queer, stop calling me a crypto-Nazi."

"Did he just call him a queer?" Weiss asked.

"Which one's the queer?" Floyd asked.

"Let's stop calling names," Howard K. tried again.

"I'll sock you in the goddamn face and you'll stay plastered!" Buckley shouted. Even in black and white, they knew he was red with rage. Schein choked on his beer. They all yelled at him to shut up. Buckley was still rolling.

"Let the author of Myra Breckinridge go back to his pornography and stop making any allusions of Nazism to someone who served in the infantry in the last war --"

That made Vidal laugh. "You were not in the infantry. As a matter of fact, you didn't fight."

Harry K.'s producers quickly threw up the film Katz and Floyd watched before, this time adding that Senator Ribicoff, nominating Senator McGovern for President that afternoon, called out Mayor Daley for "Gestapo tactics on the

247

streets of Chicago." The camera showed Daley showing Ribicoff what he thought of that. Even without sound, Katz knew Daley thought the Senator was a fucker.

Katz' shirt was drenched with sweat. His head was swirling but, for the first time in his life, he knew what he was going to do, what he had to do. Like Jarvie bolt upright in his bed, like Emmet Crowe in the middle of the riot, this was his moment of clarity. For better or worse, there was no other way.

43

At the post office Monday morning, Katz pulled Lisa's last letter from the box and re-read it one last time. When he finished, he flipped it over and wrote "Sorry. It wasn't meant to be. Love always, Jake'. Then he threw it in the box with the rest of her crap and took it to the counter. She was right about one thing, he thought. Thank God they didn't have that baby.

Fifteen minutes later, he ran up the steps and found his room. Sunlight streamed in through a wall of windows to the right. He ducked into the seat in the top row nearest the door.

"Good morning, everyone, and welcome," he heard. "Today we're going to start with a case you may of heard of, Miranda versus Arizona. Ring a bell with anyone?"

A few timid hands went up, and so did Katz'. The old man turned his way and pointed.

"Sir, do you find the Miranda case amusing?"

"No, sir."

"Then why are you smiling?"

"No reason, Professor," he said. "No reason at all."

Acknowledgments

I express my sincere thanks to the many people who helped me write this book. Special thanks go to:

Dr. Rodney Ellis, the first Chairman of Howard Theatre Restoration, Inc., whom I first met when we each took a friend at the same time to take one last look at the original Howard before it was torn down;

All my friends at the Howard Theatre Restoration Community Committee, especially Saleem Hylton and Jimi Dougans for sharing their memories of the Howard, Guitar Greg Gaskins, The Rev. Dr. Sandra Butler Truesdale, and Myla Moss;

Tina Scott Boyd, for filling me in on her mother's restaurant, Cecilia's;

Former MPD Chief Isaac Fulwood and former MPD Patrolman Ron Hampton for sharing their memories about the Department in 1968;

Dr. Bernard Demczuk for his historical perspectives on the Howard and the U Street corridor;

Dan Meth for the cover art;

Leslie Williams for the graphic design;

My wife Sandy, my children, Ben and Annie, and my mother, Edie, for all their encouragement; and

All the performers I saw and heard at the Howard who thrill and inspire me still.

21324628R00150

Made in the USA
Middletown, DE
25 June 2015